Daddy.

Her stomach dropped. This hurt a million times worse than she'd thought it would. Beck wasn't giving up and going away. She'd have to tell him the rest of Brigid's warning. Otherwise, he would never understand why she couldn't let him within ten miles of their child.

Thank goodness Dani was safely hidden.

Knowing she had to choose her words carefully, she squared her shoulders. "The Seer, Brigid, was very specific in her warning."

"The Vampire Priestess? She's also a seer?"

"Yes. Her magic is powerful and she can see things." Another deep breath. "She warned me against you and your kind."

"You don't think I…" Eyes narrowed, as he stared at her, a muscle worked in his jaw. "I would never hurt a child, especially my own daughter. She meant someone else, not me."

"More than anything, I want to believe you. But I can't take a chance. I'm sorry, but that's why I go alone. I trust no one. Not even you."

Dear Reader,

There is much to celebrate in life. Oftentimes, caught up in the daily hustle and grind, we lose sight of that. Sometimes it takes a miracle to make us recognize truly how lucky we are. I try to count my blessings daily—hourly if I remember—and even the smallest things—a perfect butterfly, a blooming flower, the way the sun colors the clouds ocher—are causes for celebration.

It's not always like that, nor will it be. I know into every life occasionally comes darkness, sweeping in and throwing a black cloak over the sun. Such is the case with my Lone Wolf, Pack Protector Anton Beck. Still mourning the loss of his sister and having given up searching for his mate, an unlikely Vampire Huntress named Marika, Beck is living a solitary life when he is granted a miracle. A daughter. Now not only are vampire/shape-shifter matches frowned upon, but since they are technically dead, Vampires are unable to bear living children. That Marika not only does this, but raises the miracle child in secret, is another thing to marvel at. That is, if Beck could see past his rage at being lied to.

Of course, a child that shouldn't exist is very valuable and is hunted, and Beck and Marika's journey to not only protect her but find and stop the ones who want to take her, is in itself something to celebrate. Love can clear back the blackest darkness and bring a spectacular ocher sunrise, if only you let it into your heart.

I hope you enjoy reading the *Lone Wolf*.

Karen Whiddon

LONE WOLF

KAREN WHIDDON

MILLS & BOON

All the characters in this book have no existence outside the imagination of the author, and have no relation whatsoever to anyone bearing the same name or names. They are not even distantly inspired by any individual known or unknown to the author, and all the incidents are pure invention.

First published in Great Britain 2011
by Mills & Boon, an imprint of Harlequin (UK) Limited,
Eton House, 18-24 Paradise Road, Richmond, Surrey TW9 1SR

© Karen Whiddon 2011

ISBN: 978 0 263 88331 2

089-1111

Harlequin (UK) policy is to use papers that are natural, renewable and recyclable products and made from wood grown in sustainable forests. The logging and manufacturing processes conform to the legal environmental regulations of the country of origin.

Printed and bound in Spain
by Blackprint CPI, Barcelona

Karen Whiddon started weaving fanciful tales for her younger brothers at the age of eleven. Amidst the Catskill Mountains of New York, then the Rocky Mountains of Colorado, she fueled her imagination with the natural beauty of the rugged peaks and spun stories of love that captivated her family's attention.

Karen now lives in North Texas, where she shares her life with her very own hero of a husband and three doting dogs. Also an entrepreneur, she divides her time between the business she started and writing the contemporary romantic suspense and paranormal romances that readers enjoy. You can e-mail Karen at KWhiddon1@ aol.com or write to her at PO Box 820807, Fort Worth, TX 76182, USA. Fans of her writing can also check out her website, www.KarenWhiddon.com.

To my husband Lonnie and my daughter Stephanie—
my own two miracles

Chapter 1

His dashboard clock showed one minute after midnight. The patrons spilling from the doorway of Addie's Bar were well into their partying, reeling around the parking lot laughing and shouting.

Anton Beck parked his truck and turned the ignition off, feeling the loud bass thump of the music all the way out here. Smoke curled from the open windows, a blue haze that reminded him of the morning mists of Vancouver Island, one of his favorite places on earth.

But this was Alpine, Texas, and even at this late hour, heat still shimmered from the dry earth in muted waves. Now that his air conditioner no longer blew, the heat made beads of perspiration break out on his forehead. He needed to get out of the truck and begin what he'd come to do.

Still he sat, unwilling yet to take the steps necessary to take him inside. A headache had begun to throb behind his eyes, the kind that promised to explode into a full-blown migraine if he wasn't careful. The noise level inside the bar just might be enough of a trigger to send him staggering for a quiet place to lie down. He hoped not. Not tonight, of all nights. Such a thing was not possible.

Swallowing, he hesitated. Once he stepped onto the gravel, he knew the memories would swirl around him, haunting him with the aching familiarity of grief. Stark contrast to the riotous nightlife going on in and around the bar.

A bar was the last place he wanted to be tonight, any night, actually. But this was a special night, and this was Addie's Place. Addie was the nearest person he had to family, and this was the closest thing he had to home. He needed to say hello to her, to let her wrap him in her flower-scented arms and hug him, while feeding him tortillas and tamales. As though her rich, sinful food could help him begin healing the scars that pockmarked his soul.

But first, he needed to focus on his sister. This night, he had a ritual to complete. He had made a small cross outside the bar, near the rise and the twisted tree. Every year he came on the same date to light a candle and stand guard over the marker that noted the spot where his baby sister, Juliet, had been killed. He'd never forgiven himself for her death. She'd been here to meet him, after all. And he'd been running late.

Growing up, he'd always wanted to watch over her, keep her safe. Being taken away by the Pack to become a Protector had made this impossible. But he'd done what he could. In this instance, he'd failed tremendously. His own mother hadn't spoken to him since.

Now, three years had passed, and each year he felt the burden of guilt heavier on his shoulders.

A group of vampires strolled past his truck, laughing quietly amongst themselves. Their pale skin gleamed in the moonlight, beautiful and icy. Beck couldn't help but admire them, even knowing that at one time in the distant past, they'd been his sworn enemy.

And, as had become habit now, he searched all their faces, compulsively seeking one that was less than perfect, yet still lovely. Marika, his sister's best friend. She'd disappeared after Juliet had died, making him wonder if she'd had something to do with her death. If he ever saw her again, he planned to ask her.

Though he'd not yet found her, he hadn't given up hope. Vampires these days humored him. Once, staring too long would have been seen as an insult and caused a battle.

Juliet had endured a lot of flack for her friendship with Marika. Shape-shifters and vampires just didn't mix.

Beck had proven this even further by his one misstep with his sister's best friend. Though Juliet had never known about their brief affair, he'd never forgiven himself. He and Marika had been together when Juliet had been killed. The memory, even now so ragged and painful, made him flinch.

Shaking off the ache in his chest and the nagging hurt in his head, Beck got out of the car. He took a deep breath, straightened his shoulders and headed toward the bar. Before he could see Addie's welcoming smile, he had a pilgrimage to make.

He patted his hunting-vest pocket, making sure his bottle of rotgut was still there. It was. Though he would have welcomed company, specifically Marika's, without her this salute was better made alone. When he'd finished, then and only then, he could go inside and accept comfort from the woman who'd loved them both like her own.

Trudging up the slight rise, he stared out over the moonlit land that seemed to go on forever, unbroken except for sagebrush and cactus. In the distance, the mesa rose, dark purple against the night sky, a tribute to ancient gods from a long-forgotten past.

He'd long ago tried to make his peace with them, settling finally for an uneasy compromise.

Each step brought him closer to hell.

Here. He slowed as he reached the spot. The marker, a stylized ankh carved in granite, had been well-tended, and someone had placed a foil-wrapped planter of tulips in front. Addie.

Beck smiled slightly, making a mental note to thank her later.

He dropped to his knees on the soft grass and pulled out his bottle, barely wetting his lips before he spoke. "Hey, Jules," he said softly. "Me again."

The answering silence felt full of condemnation.

This time, he took a swig in earnest, the pungent whiskey burning down his throat. When he'd finished, he wiped his mouth with the back of his hand. "I haven't found your killer, not yet. But I promise you I won't give up."

No answer, of course. There never was.

Beyond him, in the undulating land toward the mesa, he heard the muted sounds of nature in the night, behind him, human noises of revelry enhanced by alcohol and music.

With a sigh, he took one more slug of the whiskey. He thought of all the things he'd like to say to his sister, of everything that had happened in the past year, without her. He missed Jules, missed her badly, and, though he knew this would never bring her back, he raised the whiskey bottle to begin his third and final toast.

Something or someone slammed into him from behind, knocking the bottle out of his hand and sending whiskey flying.

Beck twisted, ready to fight. He cursed the stupidity that had made him let his guard down, cursed, too, the fact that he couldn't even mourn without some bozo wanting to prove his manhood.

More than one. There were three of them, swaying slightly from drink, felt hats pulled low to keep the moonlight from revealing their faces. Two humans and a shifter, wearing his long hair in a thick braid down his back.

Beck got in one good left hook, connecting with a satisfying crunch. He felt confident he broke that guy's jaw, before one of the others picked up his whiskey bottle and smashed him hard over the back of the head.

In the dark place where they'd confined her, Marika Tarus bit back her rage and bided her time. Eventually, her captors would grow careless. Someone would open the cement sarcophagus to check on her and then, she'd attack. She'd channel all her anger and pain into building her strength.

The rough cement no longer felt cold or hard. She allowed herself no sensations, nothing but the all-consuming fury that heated her from within. She was patient—one didn't live a few hundred years without learning that trait—and she could wait until she was given the opportunity to escape. When they did give her that chance, she'd flee. But first, she'd extract her vengeance.

All vampires knew not to mess with a Vampire Huntress. Now these stupid humans would know, too.

She moved, the tiny effort bringing a slash of pain. They'd broken her legs and shattered her kneecaps, but her body had already mostly healed. Vampires healed quickly. She'd been able to move her legs without pain after two days and, though something still felt wrong, knew she'd be able to walk once she got to her feet.

If she got to her feet. How long were they going to keep her locked up in total darkness? And for what reason? No matter what they did to her, she'd never tell them what they wanted to know.

Once she'd refused to answer their questions,

they'd beaten and tortured her, then put her into her current prison. It had taken all three of them to lift the lid and slide the massive stone over her. This was the only thing heavy enough to contain her vampiric strength. Otherwise, she'd have escaped long ago.

They'd given her injections, too—some kind of sedative. At first, the drug had knocked her for a loop, but the drowsy fog had worn off after a few hours.

The fools believed they were winning. Keeping her here, they believed if she were deprived of nourishment—blood—long enough, she'd grow weak. She'd heard them discussing how long it could be before she wasted away. Their theory was eight weeks, tops. She'd smiled grimly in the absolute darkness. They had no idea how many months a vampire of her age could go without drinking. One more advantage she'd have, were they ever foolish enough to release her.

For now, she lay in her silent prison and waited.

Confinement in the small, airless space would have made her feel claustrophobic if she'd been human. Since she was quite used to squeezing into tiny places, the prison tomb didn't bother her. Yet. No doubt they were hoping her enforced solitude would eventually drive her mad.

They didn't know, she thought, grinning savagely to herself, she'd gone mad three years ago to the day. Knowing her best friend had died in her place, because of her sins, had made her that way.

Now, she had one thing to live for. Her daughter. She'd never betray Dani, no matter what they did to her.

Beck came to trussed up like a turkey, being transported in the back of a pickup truck. With each bounce and dip of the tires, his body slammed against the metal bed. The haze of pain made him grimace, though his first thought was of Addie. She'd worry when he didn't show up for their annual remembrance.

Finally, they arrived somewhere, and the truck stopped. All three of his captors climbed in the truck bed then, standing around him as though debating their next move.

"Where is she?" One of them—the one who

was also a shifter—kicked him, hard. "Tell us, or we'll kill you both."

He grunted, glaring up at them. Blood ran in a slow trickle from a cut on his head. He itched to wipe it away, but with his hands tied, he couldn't.

She? "Who?" he managed to croak.

Instead of answering, his captor slapped him, hard enough to send his head ricocheting against the metal side.

Stars exploded and his vision blurred. While he gasped for breath, fighting against the pain, they waited, watching. One of them grinned like a fool. Beck wanted to smash that one's face in.

And he still had no idea what they wanted.

Damn. The world had gone insane. When the two other men lifted him and held him, one on each arm, Beck stared blankly at his attacker, wishing he could clear his head enough to think and plan. And change.

Instead, he stalled again, with truth. "I don't know what you're talking about."

Another punch, this time to the gut. Beck doubled over, retching.

"Where is she?" Same question, same intonation. Tell us what we want to know, or we'll torture you until you can take no more.

"Tell us. Where is she?"

"Who?" Beck cried out. "Come on, buddy. Give me a break. You have the wrong man."

The tall, wiry shifter stepped back, adjusting his hat. He wore his inky black hair in a long, braided rope down his back. Flexing his fist, he glared at Beck before addressing the others. "I think he's telling the truth."

"No, he's not." The one with the battered hat leaned closer, giving Beck a whiff of sour breath and cigarette smoke. "Let me make this clear. We've got the woman. Now, we want the kid. Either you tell us where she is, or the woman dies."

The woman? The kid? Beck closed his eyes, fighting back a wave of nausea and shock. "Listen," he said and then attempted to lick his cracked lips. "I honestly don't know what you're talking about. What woman?"

"The same one you've been looking for," the tall man spat. "The vampire bitch and her demon offspring. Your daughter."

His blood ran cold. "You must be mistaken. I have no children." He had to try, God help him, to make them realize what nonsense they were spouting. What they spoke of was impossible.

"I have no child," he repeated.

"You do. We've seen the photographs of your kid. Yours and the vampire's."

He couldn't help himself. "Come on. Surely you know that vampires can't have children. Everyone knows that."

The three men glared at him, disbelief plain in their faces.

"We're taking you to her," the shifter with the long braid said, spitting a brown wad of chewing tobacco on the ground near Beck's feet. "Maybe once you see what we're going to do to the mother of your daughter, you'll realize we're serious and tell us what we want to know."

Stepping around him, the two men shoved him out of the truck. The three-foot fall felt like a story as he hit the ground hard and lay crumpled in a heap. A moan of pain escaped him.

Ignoring this, his escorts jumped down beside him and yanked him up again, one on each side, supporting him. As they moved forward,

Beck stumbled and fell, earning a kick from the braided shifter.

"Let's go." He prodded Beck's back with something sharp that might have been a knife or a stick. This one, Beck vowed silently, rage welling up inside him, would pay later. He'd change and fight him, wolf to wolf. And when he won, he'd have no compunction about ripping out the other man's throat.

For now, he bent his head and struggled forward. One of his legs and three of his ribs felt broken. Luckily, shape-shifters healed quickly, so in a day or two, he should be good as new.

If they let him live that long.

Their nonsensical words had been exactly that—nonsense. He had no daughter. Even if such a thing were possible, Marika wouldn't have kept his own child from him.

Yet she had disappeared.… He cursed them and then himself for believing such nonsense even for a second.

They urged him forward with a shove. He drooped, pretending to be weaker than he was, stumbling for good effect.

"How much farther?" he croaked, conserving his strength for later.

Striding ahead now, braided man barely spared him a glance. Again, Beck had to clamp down his fury. Though he truly thought he could take them all, he wanted to wait and see if they really had captured Marika Tarus.

And find out if he actually had a daughter.

He grimaced because the whispering thought wouldn't go away.

"There." His captor pointed to a building, looming above them in the darkness. "We're keeping her inside the basement, in the dark where her kind belong."

Stumbling again, Beck allowed them to steer him toward the entrance, all the while keeping his wolf and his rage in check. With each step, his anticipation grew. Could it really be Marika, the same vampire woman he'd sought for the past three years? What were the odds that these men had captured the one he'd hunted unsuccessfully for so long?

A thousand to one, at least. Even higher, since they kept babbling about some mythical child.

His child. Right. Again he shrugged off the thought. One thing he'd learned over the years was how dangerous it could be to allow himself to feel hope.

Keeping his head down, he let them lead him inside, his anger building with every step, fueling him, giving him energy. He was careful to give no sign of his rapid recovery, conserving his strength for when he'd need it.

Marika heard voices, muffled and faint, through her cement prison. They'd returned, the men who kept her here, believing she'd reveal the most precious aspect of her existence. Little did they know, she'd allow them to burn her to ash in full sunlight before she'd endanger little Dani.

Then, the faint grinding as they struggled to remove the sarcophagus lid. Ah, her time had come. Their hour of reckoning.

She held her breath while it slid slowly, painfully open, inch by inch. Even though they only used one small electric lantern, the new light seared her eyes, so accustomed to inky blackness had she become.

Slowly, she adjusted, blink by blink, peering through her lashes at the blur of human faces surrounding her. She didn't move, not yet. Motionless, she bided her time, building her strength for the optimal moment to make her bid for freedom.

Then, once she was free, they would pay for daring to hold her here like this. She'd kill them all, one by one, and gorge herself in a fit of savagery on their still-warm blood, as her half-savage ancestors used to.

Just the thought gave her a burst of adrenaline.

"Get up," one of them said, a hint of nervousness in his husky voice. "We brought someone to see you."

Instantly she froze, a frisson of fear stabbing her. Not Dani, surely they hadn't found her daughter. No, she would have known, in that place in her chest where the heart of a mother once beat. Not Dani. Who, then, and why? Had they captured another vampire?

Curious despite herself, she swallowed back the rage and pushed herself to her elbows, still pretending weakness.

At first, blinking in the dim light, she counted only the same three. The tall shapeshifter with his long, dirty braid. The short man, fastidiously clean, who always smelled of coffee and soap, and the other, pudgy and mean-eyed, ever-present cigarette smoldering.

Then, she saw him. The newcomer, another shifter. So badly beaten his swollen face was barely recognizable. Sagging against the cement wall, he seemed hardly able to hold himself upright.

But when he raised his head and their gazes met, her entire world tilted crazily. Marika gasped, unable to help herself. Him! She knew this man, knew him intimately, and she'd taken care to avoid him.

Grief stabbed her, awful and swift. "You," she said. Only that, but enough. "Beck." Anton Beck, who went by his last name.

Slowly, painfully, he nodded and then gave her that lopsided smile she still remembered. "Marika, where have you been hiding? I've been looking for you for three years."

She dipped her chin, acknowledging the truth of his statement. "I know. I didn't want to be found."

One of the others made a sound, reminding her of their presence. That they should witness this, such a powerful personal moment, brought the fury back in full force. For this, too, they'd pay.

Reading her intentions in her face, Beck shook his head. "Wait," he mouthed, cautioning her as if he had the right.

The braided fool backhanded him. "Shut up. You talk when we tell you to talk."

Marika snarled, an almost wolflike growl that made Beck raise his head and go absolutely still.

She remembered how things had been between them. Hell, from the look on his face, he did, too. Explosive. Amazing. Hot and fast, furious and gentle. She'd never expected to find that with him, and fear had been part of the reason she'd run.

Dani had been the other reason.

For a moment, the harsh sound of breathing was the only noise echoing in the basement. Two of the three men, the humans, shifted their weight uneasily, sensing perhaps their impending doom. Only their leader, the shifter who'd slapped Beck, seemed impervious, arrogantly confident.

Or, she reflected grimly, stupid as hell. She'd bet on the latter.

"Here's the deal," Ponytail said. "I'm glad you know each other. Wolf-man, we're gonna let you drag vampire chick into the sun first thing in the morning. No." He held up his hand as Beck made a noise of protest. "This isn't nice, especially since we know you've been trying to find her for a long time. But she's hiding someone we want more. You know this. The two of you can put your heads together and come up with a solution. Tell us where the kid is and we'll let you go."

Marika watched Beck. Though he hadn't known about their daughter, his closed-off expression showed no hint of his thoughts.

"I'll die before I let you have her," she declared, waiting as Beck had asked, but eager to flex her returning strength and take them all down now.

"We'll let you have that wish," the shorter captor chortled. His laughter died instantly when Marika cut him a look promising retribution.

"Ten minutes." Ponytail motioned the others to follow him. "This entire room is concrete, like a bunker. There are no windows and the only door is cement also, controlled remotely by me. So don't even think of escaping. You won't be able to."

The three exited. As they did, the heavy door ground into place, closing with a thud. The meager lightbulb cast long shadows on the walls.

"Like the pyramids," she said, more to fill the silence than anything else. "Except they had only torches that went out once the oxygen left."

Swinging her legs over the side of the stone sarcophagus, she stood, swaying slightly. "You have no idea how good it feels to be out of that thing."

He came closer, studying her face with an intent look that made her shiver. "Did we—you really have a child?"

For a split second she thought of lying, but she could no longer hide. "Yes. A daughter. I named her Danielle, Dani for short."

"How is that possible?" Frowning at her, he looked unconvinced. "Vampires can't conceive."

Lifting one shoulder, she winced at the twinge of pain. "So they say. But I did. I went to speak with our seer and she told me this happens rarely. When it did, the child was meant to achieve great things. So, nine months later, my baby was born."

"Our baby," he corrected, looking shell-shocked. As he stared at her, anger gradually replaced the surprise. "You kept this from me. My daughter. Why?"

The moment she'd been dreading. Swallowing hard, she kept her gaze on him, not allowing herself the luxury of looking away. "Please. I had my reasons. I'll explain later, I promise."

From the grim set of his jaw, she could tell he didn't believe her. But finally, eyes blazing dark fury, he jerked his head in a nod.

"Is Dani a Halfling?"

Relief flooded her, which she instantly hid. She didn't pretend to misunderstand his meaning. "She can shape-shift, if that's what you mean. She's alive."

"Not a vampire." He spat the word as if he hated all of her species because of what she'd done. She didn't suppose she could actually blame him.

"No." Her short laugh sounded bitter, she knew. "I couldn't nurse her. But I bought formula and she thrived. She's two and a half years old now."

"Why do they want her?"

"That I don't know. The seer warned me while I still carried her in my womb. To protect her, I hid among my own kind, until I learned Dani wasn't safe there. Then I had no choice but to go into a human city and try to blend in. That's how they found me."

"Where is she?" His voice was a harsh whisper. "My daughter, where is she now?"

"Safe." If she'd had a heart, it would have ached. So much pain in his face, grief in his voice. He'd never forgive her for what she'd done. She told herself it didn't matter. Only Dani mattered.

"For now."

"For always." She glanced at the door, trying to judge the time. "When they come back, I'm going to kill them."

"Can you? Are you strong enough?"

"Yes."

"How long has it been since you fed?"

Again, she shrugged, forgetting her stiff shoulder. "Weeks, I think. Not long enough to hurt me. I'm fine. I'm still stronger than they."

"You need blood. Drink mine." He came closer, turning his head so his neck was exposed to her. "Use my blood to give yourself strength."

Shocked, she stared at him, while her body reacted. "You don't know what you're saying," she rasped, her mouth dry and her fangs suddenly aching. "When a vampire goes this long without nourishment, sometimes it's difficult to stop."

"But you will." His gaze met hers, his full of a confidence she didn't share. "My sister loved you and said you were strong."

"Not that strong."

Again he moved closer, bringing to her his tantalizing scent, so aromatic that she wanted to weep. "Drink. Hurry up, we don't have much time."

He hated her and yet was willing to do this for her? It made no sense.

As if he understood her thoughts, he gave her a grim smile. "Two is better than one. If we're going to get out of here, I need you strong enough to fight at my side. Now drink."

Despite her best intentions, she bent her head and moved in, ready to do as he asked.

Chapter 2

Before she could, the outer door began to grind open.

"Too late." She stepped backward, feeling only relief. Sharing blood with Anton Beck felt too intimate somehow, especially after what had happened between them.

Plus, she didn't really need it. Dark knows, she'd rested a long time. Even without feeding, she still had enough strength to take down ten puny humans.

Protecting the injured shifter might be a bit problematic, though he seemed to think he was in fighting condition. For both their sakes, she hoped so.

"How badly are you hurt?" She rushed the question.

"Not as bad as I look." Flexing his fists, he grinned at her. That grin, and the flash of attraction she felt, made her remember why she'd done what she had. Sometimes, she saw his face in her daughter's.

Pushing away her thoughts, she focused all her attention on the slowly opening door.

When the concrete slab had opened halfway, two of their three captors stepped through. Only the tall shifter with the braid was missing.

"Where's the other?" She made her voice soft, casual.

The fat one seemed nervous, pudgy fingers fidgeting with a ring of keys. "He went to get the rope."

Holding up a large cross, the dirty one grinned, showing stained teeth. "Don't even think about trying anything."

A cross. What a fool. Some of her kind had lived in the times before Christianity. Either way, a cross had no effect on her. She wanted to laugh but knew better than to reveal the truth. She'd take any advantage she could get.

Still, who were these men, and why were they living in the dark ages? Did they really think such a thing could harm her? They must not know squat about vampires. Excellent for her, bad for them.

She eyed them, letting her gaze travel down the length of them, twisting her mouth as though she found them wanting. Which she did, actually.

The smelly man began to sweat. He lifted his cross higher, trying to hide his terror. He didn't realize that she could smell it, even over the stench of his unwashed body. The pungent scent of panic made her fangs ache and her stomach clench. Suddenly starving, she wanted to feed.

But she forced herself to remain still. Though every instinct urged her to jump them—first the one with the cross, then his partner—she wanted all three to pay. She'd wait for ponytail man to return with the rope.

"I don't think he's coming back," Beck said in a casual voice. He still slumped against the wall, as though it hurt him to straighten. But she read both strength and determination in his dark eyes and knew that he, like her, only pretended weakness.

What he didn't realize was that she didn't need his help. She didn't need anyone's help.

It turned out Beck was wrong. Walking heavily, the other man returned with the rope. As he held it up, she frowned. What kind of rope was that? It looked more like snow chains for car tires, interwoven with metal links and rods for strength.

Again she had to stifle a grin. They might have been able to keep her contained with a cement sarcophagus, but these puny metal chains would hold nothing.

"Silver," the man said, holding them aloft so they clinked. "Extra protection."

"Wrong species," Beck drawled. "Vampires care nothing about silver. That's us shapeshifters. You should have made the rope out of garlic."

Marika's mouth twitched savagely at his mocking tone. The tall man suddenly appeared to have an inkling of his fate. His nostrils flared in terror, and he spun for the door, making a run for it.

Now.

Marika moved, vampire speed. Her former captor went down before he'd even taken a full step. Though by the laws of karma he should suffer, she ended his life quickly, ripping out his throat. Then, spinning before she'd even taken a satisfyingly deep drink of his warm blood, she launched herself at the other two captors, who'd frozen in shock.

Fat man screamed like a pig. Dirty man went down blubbering. Him, she killed instantly. Turning to the fat man, she began gorging herself, letting herself drink her fill of his rich blood as the life force ebbed from him.

"Enough. Let him go," Beck said, yanking her up from her feeding.

For a moment, she could only snarl up at him. Then, regaining her focus, she shook her head, sending droplets of blood flying. "I can't. I've bitten him. If I don't kill him now, he'll become a vampire."

Beck frowned. "That one's a shifter." Pointing toward the braided one with the ripped-out throat, he moved closer. "He's full-blooded, so he's not dead. He won't turn. You know our blood's immune to your bite."

"I killed him." She shrugged. "Sorry."

"No, you didn't. I just told you, he's not dead. Only silver bullets or fire can end a shape-shifter's life. Look, he's already beginning to heal."

Standing, she wiped her mouth on the back of her hand, leaving a bloody smear. "Then we'll set the place on fire."

"No." Beck pulled his cell phone from his pocket. "He's Pack. We have laws. I don't want to be an accessory to murder. Let me call Pack authorities."

Punching in a speed-dial code, he gave the information in short, staccato sentences. When he hung up, she regarded him quizzically.

"You didn't tell them where we are."

"Didn't need to. My phone's a special phone, with a GPS locater built-in. They'll use that to pinpoint this place."

"They can track you wherever you are?"

"Yeah."

"That doesn't bother you?"

He shrugged. "No. Why should it? I'm not doing anything I'd be ashamed of."

To each his own. With a nod, she bent over her victim, who'd expired quietly. Though she hadn't drunk until she was stuffed, she felt pleasantly full. Already, her veins began to buzz with renewed energy. "This one's definitely dead. Let me check the other."

A quick check of the pulse revealed that man, too, had expired. "I'm done here. Let's get out of here before your Pack people show up. I don't want to have to answer any questions."

Beck followed her as she headed for the door.

Once outside, she took deep breaths of the cooling air, enjoying her mild buzz. She wasn't used to the heady richness of fresh human blood. Like many other of her kind, she usually relied on blood banks or wild animals for nourishment.

Taking a deep breath, she turned to face her deceased best friend's older brother. "I'm gonna run."

Beck grabbed her arm. "Not yet. If you're going to wherever you have our daughter hidden, I'm going with you."

She hissed. "I'm not going there. I don't want to endanger her."

"You have to make sure she's all right."

"That's one thing I know for sure. She's safe."

"I'd prefer to check in person. It's time I met her."

Panic clogged her throat. "I can't take the chance. You don't know who might be watching me."

"I'll make sure we aren't followed. We'll go together," he said, in a tone that left no room for arguing. Behind his eyes, she glimpsed his wolf, pacing restlessly.

She let him see her fangs. "I don't think so. I go alone and in the opposite direction. Dani is safe, believe me."

For a moment, he considered her, his expression so stark she wanted to cry. Steeling herself, she lifted her chin. "I don't want to fight you. Let me go."

"Fight me?" He sounded incredulous. "Bring it on."

Suddenly remembering, she felt heat suffuse her. When they'd been together in the past, play fighting had always led to passion. Something about the adrenaline…

Three years had gone by. They'd changed.

"I don't want to fight you," she said slowly. "I just want you to leave me alone."

"We made a child, Marika. Dani. Now we're forever tied together by her."

"No." Her protest sounded weak. He ignored it, as she'd suspected he would.

"We need to talk," he insisted, as though by the strength of his voice, he could force her to give in.

He didn't realize she wouldn't, couldn't. While she wasn't ready for a physical altercation with him, she thought if she could fuel his simmering rage with her, turn it to hatred, maybe she could make him angry enough to go away. It was worth a shot.

"Oh, yeah?" Tossing her long hair back over her shoulders, she forced a smile before pulling her arm free. "There's nothing to talk about. We were over long ago. And you don't even know Dani is yours. I had lots of lovers. She could be anyone's."

He looked unconvinced and unmoved. But what did she expect? She'd always been a crappy liar. Juliet would have seen through her instantly.

"When we were together, you weren't with anyone else," he said, teeth clenched. "I know Dani is my daughter. I have a right to see her."

"I have a right to keep her alive."

He reeled back as though she'd slapped him. "I would never hurt her. How could you even think that?"

"I trust no one."

"I don't care. This isn't even between you and me, it's between me and my daughter. She has just as much right to know her father as I do to know her. Come on, Marika. You never were a fool. Stop this."

She spun away, throwing words back at him over her shoulder. "Just leave me alone. Trust me, it's better that way, for all concerned."

Easily, he kept pace with her, fury simmering in his eyes, making them appear black. "No. Where is Dani? I want to see her."

She didn't answer, knowing no matter what she said, her tone would brand her a liar.

"You can't take her away from me now that I know. I won't let you."

The rawness of his voice stung her. She knew that emotion all too well. After all, by their joining together, they'd inadvertently caused her best friend's death. Still, fool that she was, she'd missed him. Even if she'd wanted to forget him, she couldn't. Every time she'd looked at the child they'd created together, she'd seen his face. And Juliet's. She still missed her best friend, his sister. Dani's aunt.

Beck still watched her, silently waiting.

Abruptly, she wondered how he'd dealt with his sister's loss. Then she wondered why she cared. She couldn't afford to care about anything, anyone else but Dani. And keeping her safe trumped what anyone else wanted, including herself. Especially herself.

Yet that knowledge didn't make it any easier to do what she had to do—try and make him hate her enough to leave.

"Why? Why do you care? You never even wanted kids. Why do you suddenly want one now?" With fresh blood humming through her veins and giving her strength, she faced him, well aware how intimidating she could look in her full vampire glory.

But he was a shape-shifter—vampires didn't threaten him. Never taking his gaze from her face, his eyes had gone cold and flat. "That was in the past. What I wanted then has nothing to do with any of this. Dani was conceived and born. I would have given my wolf to be there for that. No matter."

"No matter?" She could scarcely believe his words.

"Make no mistake. I don't like what you did and I may never forgive you for that. But Dani is all that matters now. She's just as much mine as yours. I want to see her, get to know her. You've already deprived me of two entire years of her life."

Pain made her temples ache and her throat tight. He was right, but she'd had no choice. She still had no choice. There were no words to answer him. She slowed her frantic pace. No matter that he was right, this was out of her hands. She had to protect her baby. No matter the cost to either of them.

His sensual mouth twisted. "Answer my question. Where is she?"

She hadn't answered, nor would she, as long as she could stall him. She knew deep down in her bones that if he saw Dani, he'd take one look at her tiny, perfect face, and he'd never leave. Once, Beck had staked a claim on her. The idea that he wanted to make a claim on her little girl terrified her. Both because of what she knew and something else, a tiny, selfish part of herself that she didn't much like.

Inhaling, she tried to get her second wind. "What gives you the right to know anything about me or mine? Despite our mistake three years ago, we're actually strangers, with only Juliet in common."

"Mistake?" For the space of a second he dipped his chin, the movement slight and barely noticeable, but enough to tell her how much her words hurt him.

"I—"

His lip curled. "What gives me the right? That you can ask such a question tells me my sister didn't know you as well as she thought."

She felt his words like a knife.

"Don't," she said. "You know nothing about me—"

"I've lost my sister. She was all I had left in the world. Yes, you were her best friend. And maybe what happened between us never should have happened. But it did, and we made a child together."

Again she tried to speak, knowing he was right, but also aware she had to try. The words wouldn't come.

"I have the right to know her," he continued. "She's my blood as much as yours, my family, my child, too." His voice broke, but the accusation in his eyes cut her like shards of broken, lethal glass.

Head aching, she tried to think. His child. Their child. Dani.

Taking a deep breath, she wondered if she'd be able to convince him or if she was simply wasting her breath. Finally, she shook her head, sending her long hair flying. She had no choice but to continue to try. Especially taking into account the High Vampire Priestess's warning.

Bravely, she lifted her chin. "All I'm asking for is the chance to raise my daughter in peace."

"Raise your— She's mine, too, Marika. Mine. It's bad enough you didn't think I had the right to know when she was born."

"For her own safety." The words exploded from her. "I couldn't tell you. I've been warned. They've been after me from the beginning."

He went utterly still. Finally, he was listening. "You keep alluding to her safety. If you're telling the truth, tell me this. Who's been after you?"

"I don't know." Even to herself, her admission sounded weak, contrived. Still, he was a Protector, sworn to protect his own kind. She couldn't tell him what he wanted to know without risk. And if she did, she was certain he would think she was lying.

"Come on." His gaze raked her face. "You're looking for excuses."

Lifting her chin, she let him read the despair in her face. "Beck, I can't prove anything to you. Take my word for it. Dani's in danger. I keep her hidden to protect her. I want her safe."

"You know what? I honestly do believe you." Dragging a hand across his eyes, his voice roughened. "I don't know why, but if you think she's truly in danger, then she is. Hellhounds. Let me help you."

Stunned, she could only stare. She'd done nothing to earn his trust and everything to make him brand her a liar. Once she would have killed to have him say those words to her. Now, he represented both the past she tried so hard to forget, and danger.

"How you must hate me." Eyes tearing, Marika turned away so he wouldn't see.

"Look at me," he ordered.

Slowly, she turned, wiping at her eyes. Her breath caught as she did as he asked. Even now, she found him beautiful. With his shaggy black hair and intricate tattoos, he looked edgy and more like a vampire than she.

Leaning forward, he spoke earnestly. "Marika, I've never blamed you for what happened. I blamed myself. I loved my sister. For the rest of my life, I'll have to deal with the fact that I wasn't there when she needed me. I failed to protect her."

"Because you were with me."

He dipped his chin, acknowledging the truth of her words, and the lie. "We both know it was wrong, but there was no way we could have predicted what happened."

"Juliet paid the ultimate price." With nothing left to give him but the truth, she kept her voice steady. "Dani resulted from that night. Life from death. I would have thought you would hate her."

"Do you?" His hard voice made her flinch. "Do you hate her?"

She frowned. "Don't be ridiculous. Of course I don't hate my daughter. What happened to Juliet wasn't Dani's fault, it was mine—ours. Dani was the only thing that kept me sane."

"There." He pounced on her words. "Don't you see? I've fought my own battles with grief, with guilt over what happened. I would have welcomed Dani, loved her, let her save me, too, if you'd given me the chance."

She refused to allow him to make her feel any guiltier than she already felt. He didn't know what she knew. "I told you, I couldn't. I was telling the truth earlier. She's in danger. I couldn't let anyone find out about her. Not my own people and certainly not yours." She clamped her lips together in a straight line.

"Why certainly not mine?"

"For her own safety. And, Beck, I didn't do what I did out of malice. I honestly didn't know how you would feel about her, and worse, I couldn't take the chance of trying to find out. Surely you can understand that."

"No, I can't." His eyes narrowed. "Tell me what happened. That night, after we found Juliet…"

"I waited for you. When you didn't return, I

drove to Addie's bar. The police were already there. When I learned what had happened, I knew. I searched for you, but couldn't find you anywhere. Then I looked for Addie, but she'd disappeared, too. Someone told me you'd both gone to talk to the police." She put her hand to her mouth, wondering if the pain and grief would ever lessen.

He must have felt the same. For a moment, he bowed his head. Then, swallowing, he seemed to force himself to go on. "When I got back, you were gone. You vanished. Why? Where did you go?"

"Hunting. I went to find the ones that killed her."

"Vampire Huntress. Your skills are rumored to be unparalleled. Did you find them?"

"No." She felt a shiver of remembered rage. "For the first time in centuries, I failed. I wasn't even able to find a single clue."

"Neither did the police, whether human or shifter. Still, even if you were hunting, even if you didn't succeed, I don't understand why you hid yourself from me."

The time had come to tell him the truth.

"While I was hunting, someone else was looking for me."

"Who?"

"Brigid. She's ancient, one of the oldest of our kind. She's also a Vampire Priestess, the leader of the order of Vampire Huntresses. She's the one who told me I was pregnant. She called it a miracle." She didn't tell him what else Brigid had said. Not yet. She'd give him truth, but in bits and pieces.

"She was right. You getting pregnant is kind of a miracle. Who knew vampires could conceive a living child?"

"I certainly didn't. But Brigid also warned me that I couldn't take risks with my baby's safety. She warned me of a threat, though she didn't know when and from where it would come. I went into hiding to ensure that no one knew. No one except Brigid and Addie."

"Addie?"

"Yeah." Her voice softened. "Even though she's human and a couple of centuries younger, she's always treated me like a daughter. I trust her."

"I do, too." They shared a smile. Marika looked away first.

"Anyway," she continued. "Dani was born in an old cabin high in these mountains. I had no one to assist me, because I trusted none. Still, somehow they—whoever they are—found out. Someone came hunting. Even though she was only a few weeks old, I knew they wanted my baby."

"They?" While he wanted more detail, he didn't appear to doubt her. Yet.

"They wanted to harm her because of what she is, a child of a vampire and a shifter." Lifting her chin, she steeled herself to meet his dark gaze.

"I don't understand. So she's a Halfling. The Pack is made up of hundreds of thousands of those."

"Vampires don't have children."

"You did," he insisted. "And if you did, others can. Maybe you just haven't heard about them. Maybe your precious Brigid made them go into hiding, too."

"Maybe." Since she hadn't told him everything, she was willing to concede that point, even if she privately found it ridiculous. "Either way, protecting her comes first."

"True." He cocked his shaggy head. "But

I still don't understand why they want our daughter."

"Why doesn't matter. They want her and that's enough. I won't let them have her. Dani's everything to me."

Expression sober, he nodded. Something about the vulnerable look in his eyes brought memory slamming into her. She remembered how she'd felt when he'd held her in his strong arms, how tenderly he'd held her. How easily she could imagine him holding his daughter, laughing down into her perfect little face, so similar to his.

Fool. Such visualizations were nothing but dangerous to her now.

Unaware of her thoughts, he continued. "You know you're going to have to tell her who I am when I meet her. I don't want her thinking I'm just some guy. I want her to call me Daddy."

Daddy. Her stomach dropped. This hurt a million times worse than she'd thought it would. Beck wasn't giving up and going away. She'd have to tell him the rest of Brigid's warning. Otherwise, he would never understand why she couldn't let him within ten miles of their child.

Thank goodness Dani was safely hidden.

Knowing she had to choose her words carefully, she squared her shoulders. "The seer, Brigid, was very specific in her warning."

"The Vampire Priestess? She's also a seer?"

"Yes. Her magic is powerful and she can see things." Another deep breath. "She warned me against you and your kind."

If she'd accused him of wanting to murder their daughter, she didn't think she could have shocked him more.

"You don't think I…" Eyes narrowed as he stared at her, a muscle worked in his jaw. "I would never hurt a child, especially my own daughter. If your priestess said Pack, she meant someone else, not me."

"How could I know that?" She felt as if the words were torn from her. "More than anything, I want to believe you. But I can't take a chance. I'm sorry, but that's why I go alone. I trust no one. Not even you."

Now he cocked his head, looking wild and stern and hurt and wickedly beautiful, all at once. "That's not entirely true. You trusted someone. Where'd you leave our daughter? She's too young to be left alone."

Ah, he was right. Still, she couldn't afford to give in. "That's different."

"Oh, yeah? How?"

"All right." She waved a hand impatiently. "There is one person I trust. Dani is safe with her."

"One person you trust. Someone who would never betray you, who loves you like a daughter." He stared, the anger that had bloomed in his rugged face slowly giving way to horror.

Seeing, she couldn't help but be afraid. "What is it? What's wrong?"

"I know," he rasped. "I know where Dani is. It's Addie, isn't it? You left her with Addie?"

Her silence was its own form of answer. Though she stood perfectly still, his reaction terrified her. That, and the fact he'd been able to guess the truth, made her want to steal a car and drive straight to Addie's place.

"Dani is safe." Her words were more to comfort herself than anything else. "She *has* to be safe."

"Hellhounds," he cursed. "I'm not a hundred percent sure of that. We've got to get to Alpine, fast."

"Alpine? Addie's at my place, out in the desert."

"No, she's not. She was at the bar last night."

"Why?" She had to fight to keep herself still. The back of her neck prickled, and inside, every cell vibrated in panicked response to the urgency in his voice. Then, before he could answer, she knew. "Juliet's death."

"Yes. Every year Addie and I have our own private remembrance."

Thinking furiously, she tried to deny the possibility. "Even if Addie brought Dani to the bar, she knows to keep her safely hidden. What makes you think something happened?"

"Because they were there. That's where these goons captured me. Outside Addie's bar, at Juliet's grave. If they go back, there's a good chance they'll stumble across our daughter."

Chapter 3

"They won't go back." Even to her own ears, her declaration sounded weak. "They won't."

"I hope not." He swore. "They don't have a reason to, but what if there were more of them? Reinforcements, waiting until they got the answer they wanted."

Dani's location.

It made an awful, horrible kind of sense. Her stomach sank.

Still, she had to protest. "Even if they did have backup, why would they go there, to Addie's?"

"Addie's is the only bar of its kind in the

area, you know that. Shifters and vampires hang out there, alongside the oblivious humans. It's a meeting place. Hell, we met there. Where better to wait for news from the ones who captured us?"

"You've got to be wrong. You'd better be wrong." She took a deep, shaky breath, gripping one hand with the other so tightly it hurt, terror knotting inside her. "You have to be."

Expression grim, he felt in his pocket, bringing out his phone. Opening it, he punched in a code. "I'm calling her cell. Maybe I am wrong. If she answers, we'll know."

If she answered. She tried to force herself to relax. No if. Of course Addie would answer.

But as the silence grew, Beck holding the phone to his ear, she began to worry she wouldn't.

Trying not to shake as awful images built in her mind, Marika watched, waiting, willing Addie to answer. Which she would. Any second now. She had to. The alternative was unacceptable.

After a moment, Beck shook his head. Closing the phone, he shot her a bleak look. "No answer."

Everything seemed to freeze at exactly that moment. She tried to clear her head, to force herself to move, to do something, say something, anything—but she couldn't even force air past the blockage in her throat.

Finally, one word of protest escaped her. "But—"

He touched her, lightly. "Don't panic. There could be a thousand reasons why she didn't answer. We'll try her again later."

She nodded. A thousand reasons. Right.

Despite his assurances, panic clogged her throat. Icy fear twisting around her insides, she felt worse than dead, immobilized, horror-struck. She couldn't seem to make her voice work, though she wanted to talk, to convince herself even now that she had no reason to worry. She couldn't seem to do much more than take quick shallow breaths and try to keep from screaming.

Finally, still clenching her hand so tightly her nails dug into her palm, she forced more words past the knot in her throat. "Okay. I'm sure everything's all right. Maybe Addie left the bar and went back to my place. Or maybe she never left, and stayed at my house. It could be she decided not to make Juliet's remembrance ceremony with you this year. She might have, you know."

"Call your house." He held out his phone.

"I can't." She shook her head. "I don't have a phone there. Too easy to trace. If I need to contact her, I use Addie's cell."

Which he'd just tried, with no answer. Still trying to keep from absolutely freaking out, she looked at him.

"Beck, we can't be all that far from the bar. Just to make sure—"

"We've got to go there now," he finished for her, his deep voice calm and reassuring.

"Exactly." Finally, she could move again. Take action. In the driveway, a nondescript black pickup was parked.

Perfect.

Beck made it to the vehicle a second after she did, proving that shifters could move fast, too.

"I'm driving," he said.

She didn't bother to protest. She was too shaky to function normally and would only be a danger behind the wheel.

As they climbed in, and she settled in her

seat, buckling herself in, he gave her shoulder a gentle squeeze. "I'm sure everything's all right."

She wasn't. Hell, she couldn't even summon a fake smile. Knowing her extremely fragile control quivered on the verge of shattering, she focused on details. "Do you have any idea where we are, how far we are from Alpine? For all I know, they could have driven us into Mexico."

"I think we're still in Texas. Though I was in and out of consciousness when they brought me here, it didn't seem like we drove that long. And I'd remember if we'd stopped at the border, which would have been really risky with me tied up in the bed of the pickup."

"What about your phone? Can't you use your GPS to find out where we are?"

"I don't want to take any chances of drawing any attention to ourselves."

"Good point." Aware he was making small talk to try and keep her calm, she pointed, noting how her hand shook. "The keys are in the ignition."

"I'm thinking they didn't worry about thieves out here." His calm, even voice made her want to lash out at him. But inside, she knew he was right. A Huntress out of control was a dead Huntress. If Dani was in danger, Marika knew she needed to keep her wits about her.

"Are you okay?" he asked.

She nodded. "Good to go."

Starting the engine, Beck put the truck in Drive and pulled out. The black silence inside her gnawed away at her confidence. All she could do was yearn for her baby girl.

As though he somehow sensed this, he indicated the eastern horizon, where the lightening of the sky had been painted with broad brush-strokes of pink, red and orange.

"Looks like the sun will be coming up soon. Guess it's gonna be a scorcher."

Small talk. Small talk. Gratefully, she clung to the idea, knowing she had to regain and then maintain her composure. "Last night, do you have any idea what time they grabbed you?"

"A little after midnight." He shook his head. "We couldn't have driven too far, though time flies when you drift in and out of consciousness."

Leaning forward, she peered at the speed-ometer. Eighty. "Can't we go any faster?"

"I've got it floored. This is as fast as this beat-up old truck will go."

Not fast enough. Just thinking of Dani being captured, of their hands on her soft white skin—rough and hurting—shattered her.

"Marika." Beck's sharp tone brought her out of her dark reverie. "Stay with me."

He was right. Grateful, she nodded. "I'm here. It's just—"

"Don't go there." Fear and anger glittered in his eyes, but his voice sounded even and composed. "We were talking about how they grabbed us. I was at Addie's. What about you? Where'd they get you?"

Deep breath. And another. Drawing on years of training, she managed to keep her voice steady. "In Lubbock. I had an assignment there, which is why I had Addie come stay with Dani."

"What happened? How'd they get you?" His quiet questions contained no condemnation that she, a Huntress, had let herself be captured. But then, how could he, a Protector, condemn her when the very same thing had happened to him?

She sighed. "They set me up. I suppose I should have seen it coming, but I didn't think they had the brains to come up with such a plan. I'd completed my assignment but hadn't taken the time to feed. They doped up a goat, then hit it with a car, knowing I'd come across it in a few minutes. It was still alive when I found it. I was hungry, so…" She shrugged. "I put it out of its misery."

"And whatever they'd given it got to you through its blood."

Because there was little she could say, she settled for a quick nod, still trying to keep panic at bay.

Beck's deep voice became her lifeline. "How long were you held in the basement of that house?"

"How long? I don't know." Though the landscape flew past, the hands on the dashboard clock seemed to barely move.

"Try to think," he urged. "I need you with me, a hundred percent."

"They kept me closed up inside a stone box. It was extremely dark in there, with no way to keep track of time. If I were to give it my best guess, I'd say a couple of weeks."

While Dani had been left with Addie, safe at Marika's house. Not in the open, unprotected, at Addie's bar. Even if it had been the anniversary of Juliet's death, what had Addie been thinking?"

"Did Addie know?"

Blankly, she brought her gaze back to focus on his face. "Know what?"

"That you'd been captured?"

"No. Though I'm sure she must have figured it out when I didn't come back as promised. I couldn't let her know I was being followed—I couldn't risk giving away my house's location. I was careful not to contact her since I was being tracked. I didn't want to take a chance that they were monitoring me that closely."

"Your house is well-hidden?"

"Yes." She choked back a cry. "No one knows where I live, even Addie. When I brought her there, I was careful. I blindfolded her, made sure no one followed us."

"But she left to meet me at the bar."

"You don't know that for certain." Lashing at

him with her voice, she reached for his phone. "Maybe she decided to skip it this year."

With a slow shake of his head, he let her know what he thought of that.

"Either way, no one should have any idea that she's with Dani. If she had to go to the bar to meet you, she would have known enough to keep Dani hidden and safe."

"Which no doubt she is. We're probably worrying over nothing."

More than anything, she hoped that was true. But even though she no longer knew Beck very well, she could hear the ring of falseness in his voice.

After all, if everything was okay, why didn't Addie pick up her phone?

As if he sensed her thoughts, he reached over and gave her shoulder an awkward, quick pat. "It'll probably be all right. Even though we can't be too far, I want to keep calling her from the car. Maybe she'll eventually answer."

Maybe. But her jangling nerves insisted Addie wouldn't. Something was wrong. Very, very wrong.

"I need to talk to her, too," Beck continued. "She's bound to wonder what happened to me last night. I've never stood her up, not once in the three years since Juliet died. If she did come to meet me, I don't want her to worry."

When Marika didn't reply, he gave her a curious glance. "You and Juliet were close. What did you do to remember her death?"

The change of subject didn't fool her. Still, because she knew she'd be of no use to her daughter if she didn't get herself under control, she gratefully took the bait. "I tried not to think about it. When I remember Jules, I want to remember her alive. Vibrant. She was a shifter. She shouldn't have died. You know as well as I do that most people don't load their guns with silver bullets. I think she was murdered intentionally." She was opening a can of worms, but there it was—out there on the seat between him.

Rather than protesting, he only gave a quick nod. "Could be. Jules never did anything to deserve death. Like you, I searched for her killers."

"And you didn't find them, either. At least you have your organization's vast resources."

"I was a Protector." His dark tone told her what he thought about that. "I'm not anymore."

"You resigned?"

"Yeah. I take it you're still a Huntress."

"Of course. That's why I had to leave Dani—I had a mission." A mission she'd regret to this day. "You know, maybe it's time to think about leaving the organization. At least until Dani is grown."

He grunted, concentrating on keeping the truck on the rutted road while flooring the accelerator.

"Dani has to be okay," she said fervently. "She has to."

"Think about something else." He shot her a grim look. "Have you ever visited Juliet's memorial?"

Somehow she knew this question was important to him. "Yes, of course I have. I bring flowers with every new season. Jules loved flowers." She took a deep breath. "You meet Addie every year for a remembrance? Why?"

"Because she was the last person to see my sister alive." He gave her a lopsided smile tinged with pain. "And because, just like you, Addie is like a mother to me."

"A lot of people feel that way about her." Again her thoughts returned to her little girl.

Grabbing his phone off the console, she hit re-dial, listened to twenty-two rings without an answer before hitting the Off button and drop-ping the cell back in its place.

Beck didn't comment. "Addie introduced us, remember?"

More diversionary tactics. Normally, she'd shy away from these types of memories. But now, welcoming the distraction, she let herself be swept along, back to the past. "Of course I remember. We met there, at her bar, on Fat Tuesday. I'd gone with a bunch of other Hunt-resses, and you were alone at the bar."

"I was waiting for you. Addie had told me about you." Though he spoke in a calm, unaf-fected voice, Beck gripped the steering wheel so hard his knuckles showed white, proving his control was as ragged as hers.

"You didn't mind that I was a vampire, either."

"Just like you didn't care that I was Pack."

"At first I did." But then she'd seen him. One look and she'd been hooked. Bouncing along on a potholed road, she wondered if they'd still be together if things had been different. "Once I met you, that didn't seem to matter."

Beck glanced at her, expression serious. "We were kind of radicals, with our mixed relationship. My Pack friends gave me hell, though once they saw you, they were probably only jealous. What did your friends think of you taking up with a shifter?"

Though the speedometer inched past eighty, the landscape hadn't changed. They were in the middle of nowhere, still miles from town and Addie's.

"Marika?" His tone was sharp. "I need you to focus. What did your friends think of our relationship?"

Bringing her attention back to him, she understood what he was trying to do, though she couldn't help but wonder at his choice of topic. For her, this was all still painful. She guessed that, for him, the three years that had passed had eased the hurt.

"They weren't too happy." She shrugged. "But what can you do? You like who you like."

Like was putting it mildly. She'd never put into words what he'd made her feel. When she'd first seen Beck, everything else had faded into insignificance. The sight of his face, so ruggedly beautiful, had made her feel complete for the first time in her very long life.

"What about since then?" His casual voice didn't fool her for a second. "Has there been anyone else?"

"Not of any importance. Dani has been my only priority." Taking a deep breath, vibrating with panic, she dared to ask him the same questions. "What about you? You've never been in love?"

His hard look dismissed her question. "That's not in the cards for me."

A few more miles. A bit closer. She glanced at the phone. "Try again."

He did, finally closing it without commenting.

She swallowed. Hard. Grasped at straws, desperate for distraction. "Me, either. I haven't really tried. Don't want to."

After Beck, when their disastrous relationship had ended with his sister's death, she'd known she'd never let herself care about anyone so strongly again.

How long ago that all seemed now. Meeting Beck that night, when his eyes had locked with hers, she'd known she'd been waiting for him all her life. She'd wanted to ask him where he'd been, what had taken him so damn long to find her. He'd brought color to her world. Everything had been gray until he'd shown up.

Now, Dani was her color, her reason for existing.

She swallowed again, awash in emotion, hovering on the razor edge of terror. Dani, Dani, Dani. Her daughter had to be all right.

"Try Addie again."

Though barely a minute had passed since his last attempt, without questioning, he did.

A moment later he closed the phone and shook his head. "Still no answer."

A moan escaped her. "Bloody hell. If anything—"

"No. She's fine. I'm sure we're worrying for nothing." He sounded confident, certain.

How she wished she could agree. But every instinct told her he was wrong. She bit back a second moan.

"Marika, look at me."

Slowly, reluctantly, she dragged her gaze from her intense study of the landscape to his face.

His reassuring grin took her breath away,

suddenly and unexpectedly making his craggy face beautiful. "Don't worry. Not yet. One thing I have learned in my time as a Protector is to wait until I have all the facts. Doing otherwise just brings trouble. We don't want that."

"No," she said slowly. "But I can't ignore my instincts."

"You'd better. You know how hard it is to fight when you can't focus."

Damn. He was right. She knew this. "It works when you're not emotionally involved, but this is my daughter."

"Our daughter," he corrected. "And you worrying about her isn't going to help her if she's in trouble."

Taking a deep breath, she made herself continue to study him. Distraction, distraction. "You know," she said slowly, considering, "I'd forgotten how beautiful you are. Does that ever get in the way of what you have to do as a Protector?"

"Former Protector. And, Marika, you can't go around saying things like that." His voice sounded thick. The faint reddish tinge under his skin told her he didn't take well to compliments.

No matter. As soon as she reached Addie's, barring a disaster, she planned to take Dani and run. If things went well, she'd never see him again. Though he was Dani's father, she couldn't take a chance on letting him endanger her.

Assuming she wasn't already in danger.

She gave herself a mental shake. Everything *had* to be all right. They'd get to Addie's, wake her up, find Dani and while Beck was distracted, she'd take Dani and disappear.

Dani had to be safe. She had to be. The alternative simply wasn't acceptable.

Again she focused on her plan. Take Dani and run. If there was a way she could keep Beck away from her... The less complicated she could keep their lives, the quicker escape she and Dani could make if it became necessary to make one. Beck would only get in the way.

Dani's father. A niggling of guilt still bothered her. Casting him a sideways glance, she knew he wouldn't give up easily. Separating from him would be best accomplished quickly, before he had a chance to stop them.

Not only would Dani be safer without him,

but the truth of the matter was that being around him brought too much pain. She'd never forgotten him or understood how she'd let herself come to care for him so much, so quickly. Being with him reminded her too much of what she'd lost. Even now, the carefully constructed shield she'd put around her emotions was cracking.

Cracks were dangerous.

"This intersection looks vaguely familiar." Beck slowed to read the sign facing the other direction. "U.S. 90," he read. "Marathon, ten miles."

Close. They were getting closer. She leaned forward. "So we're heading the right way."

"Yeah. We're in between Alpine and Marathon."

Heart pounding, Marika sat up straight in the seat. "Then step on the gas. The quicker we get there, the better."

The landscape—flat scrub brush, tumbleweeds and dry, brown grass tinged silver in the moonlight—flew past them as the truck sped down the road. For the most part, Beck managed to avoid ruts; when he didn't, they bounced so hard she felt as if her teeth were going to go through the roof of her mouth.

Her stomach churned. "Try Addie again," she blurted.

"Here." He handed her the cell. "You try. Just hit redial."

She did, letting it ring twenty-seven times before closing the phone. Her feeling of foreboding increased. "Still no answer."

"We'll be there soon enough."

Not for the first time, Marika wished there was some truth to the legend about vampires being able to turn into bats and fly. If she could, she would have done so.

Finally, ahead she saw the glow of Addie's neon sign, the peculiar and familiar shade of bright pink lighting up the still-dark sky. As they neared, she saw only one familiar car in the parking lot.

"Addie's Prius." Relief flooding her, Marika couldn't keep the satisfaction from her voice. "She's still here."

"But why?" Beck pointed toward the bar. "It looks like the place is locked up tight."

"Everything looks normal." Marika softened the sharpness of her reply. "She must be inside, working. Or sleeping. She keeps a cot there. I'm guessing that's where Dani sleeps while Addie tends to the bar."

Beck killed the headlights before turning into the parking lot. Then, the engine. Coasting to a stop next to Addie's car, he put the truck in Park.

Out in a flash, Marika forced herself to wait impatiently for Beck. He grabbed her arm just as she was about to dash forward, making her stumble.

"Wait."

"Why?" She shook him off, clenching her jaw. "I want to see my daughter."

"Our daughter," he corrected. Head up, his nostrils flared. "Something's off. The scent… the air doesn't taste right."

A frisson of fear stabbed her, which she instantly pushed away. Being friends with Juliet had taught her that a shifter's sense of smell was four hundred times stronger than a human's—or a vampire's for that matter.

If he said that the scent was off, then she believed him. But she hoped to hell he was wrong.

In case he wasn't, she did as he asked and let him lead the way.

Moving cautiously, he kept close to the side of the squat brick building. His powerful, lean body moved with easy grace, yet even so close to her, there was an air of isolation about him.

"Do you see anything?" she whispered, fighting the urge to simply dash around him and inside. But if there was a chance, however small, that she might endanger Dani with rash actions, she couldn't take it.

Beck shot her a grim look. "Not yet. But the smell is getting worse."

She sniffed but detected nothing. "Do you have a weapon?"

"No. Those idiots took my gun. And I have a feeling I'm going to need it."

At this, she felt the first prickle of real alarm. Inside, she began a running litany, over and over—something she might have once called a prayer. *Let Dani be all right, let Dani be all right. Please.*

As Beck's broad shoulders disappeared around the corner and she prepared to follow, she couldn't shake the sudden, horrible sense that he was right. Something had gone terribly wrong. She could only hope Dani hadn't been hurt. She had to dig her nails into her palms to keep from rushing inside to find out.

Patience. Prudence. Caution. Words every highly trained Huntress—and Protector—knew well. And yet when someone she loved was in danger, each and every one of them became meaningless, empty.

When they reached the back side of the building and she saw the back door swinging open in the slight breeze, she froze in terror and let out a quiet moan.

Dani. Dani. Dani.

Caution be damned. She brushed past Beck.

Intent on the door, Beck raised his arm to block her. Then, with a leap that seemed more wolf than man, he crashed inside, Marika close on his heels.

Chapter 4

As his eyes adjusted to the darkness, Beck smelled the coppery, bitter scent of blood. From the sharp hiss behind him, he knew Marika detected it, too.

Blood and sweat and the tangy smell of fear.

Not good. Not good at all.

He fumbled for the light switch, flicked it on. The room looked as if a tornado had torn through it—overturned furniture, books and papers scattered everywhere, and blood. A storm of blood, drops splattering the floor and walls. Whoever had been injured here had fought violently and left a crimson trail. Most likely, this had been Addie.

She'd lost a lot of blood. He wondered if she still lived. The fact that they hadn't left her body here meant she most likely had.

"Where is she?" Marika's voice rose. "Dani? Addie?"

Biting his tongue because he didn't want to tell her they were already too late, he shook his head, knowing she'd figure things out soon enough. The blood, the wrecking of the office, all were proof.

Addie was gone. They'd taken her—and Dani, the daughter he'd never met. The idea that he had a two-year-old daughter blew his mind. The thought that Marika could have kept her existence a secret hurt more than he could have believed possible. To think he'd once thought Marika could be his mate…what a fool he'd been.

For survival's sake, he pushed the thought away for later, concentrating on the here and now. Saving Dani.

"I'll kill the bastards." Before his eyes, Marika seemed to morph into another persona, that of a Vampire Huntress, standing taller and more menacing. Larger, somehow. "When I find them, if they have harmed one hair on Dani's head, I'll tear them apart limb by limb."

Picking up the desk phone, which had miraculously escaped the bloodbath, Beck held the receiver to his ear. The dial tone buzzed, satisfyingly loud. "The phone still works, but I'm going to use my cell, just in case someone's watching this line." Retrieving his cell phone from his pocket, he punched in a series of numbers from memory.

"Who are you calling? Surely you know better than to call the local police." Marika sounded both shaken and pissed off.

"I do," he told her, listening as the call went through a complicated series of relays. "And we need to clean this place up and put a closed sign on the door. No sense in humans poking their noses around in our business."

Punching in one final code, Beck closed his phone, steeling himself as he turned to face her. The haunted look on her beautiful face made his chest hurt. "I called one of my friends, a Protector named Simon. If anyone can help us, he can. I'm sure he'll call me back shortly."

With Brigid's warning ringing in her ears, she touched his arm. "Fine, but whatever you do, don't tell him about Dani. If he knows about her, he'll want to kill her, too."

Staring at her, he slowly shook his head. "Why do you keep saying that? I don't understand your logic. Our daughter is a miracle."

One single, red tear ran down her cheek, which she promptly wiped away. "Thank you for that. I agree, yes, Dani is a miracle to me. But to everyone else, she's a freak of nature, something that shouldn't ever have been born."

When he started to contradict her, she held up her hand. "Believe me, I speak truth." She took a deep breath, regarding him steadily. "The less they know about her, the better. She's only safe if she can blend in with humans."

Beck wasn't sure he bought into that, especially since he still sensed she was hiding something. She might have received a few isolated death threats from a couple of whackos. Maybe vamps were a bit more unforgiving than shifters.

"That's where I think you're wrong." He kept his voice firm. "Maybe you have to worry about vampires, but not shifters."

"I worry especially about shifters," she said darkly.

"Look, Dani is not human. She's Pack. A Halfling. And Pack protects our own. We don't want to kill them."

"Oh, yeah? I heard about what happened with the Protectors and what you shifters called Ferals. You guys were gunning them down left and right."

He winced, feeling a stab of remorse. But only for a second, because while he was as guilty as the rest, in his heart he knew he'd already paid his own penance.

"That's over now. It was an isolated incident, during a fixed span of time. It's in the past. We rebelled against the corrupt leaders who gave the orders. It will never happen again."

With her head cocked and her arms crossed, she didn't appear to believe him. "Regardless, promise me you won't tell them about Dani."

"Marika—"

"No. This is not negotiable. Give me your word you won't say anything."

With a sigh, he gave in. "Fine. You leave me no choice."

Her gaze searched his face. Finally, she dipped her chin. "I'll take that as your word."

"You have it." He gestured with his phone. "Isn't there someone you want to call for help?"

"No."

"No Huntresses? Maybe we can ask their help. I've heard amazing things about your organization."

"Oh, yeah? That we're good at search-and-destroy missions?"

"Surely you did more than that?"

"Not really. Let me ask you this. What was your motto when you were a Protector?"

"Protect and Defend. Kind of ironic, after what happened, but the original purpose was noble. Is noble, now."

"As a Vampire Huntress, our motto was—is—Hunt and Destroy. See the problem? If the Huntresses find out about Dani, they won't rest until they kill her."

"That makes no sense."

"Sorry."

Beck couldn't believe his ears. "You know," he said slowly, "I thought I was cynical. But you've got me beat."

"I'm not cynical. I'm a realist."

"How can you not realize our daughter is the

ultimate proof that our two species can coexist in harmony? How can anyone not realize that?"

Her lip curled. "Take off your rose-colored glasses."

This cynicism saddened him, though he didn't know why. He'd felt the same himself, until now. But knowing he had a daughter, knowing about his child, Dani, had given him fresh hope. "Juliet would have told you the same if she'd lived."

She bared her teeth, a curiously Pack gesture that she must have learned from Juliet. "Don't you dare throw her in my face. I knew her as well as you."

"Really?" He raised a brow. "We were close."

"I know. But we were friends a long time. Jules would have wanted to protect Dani at all costs. I'm sorry, but..." Touching her throat as though it had closed, she swallowed hard. "I've been dealing with this a long time."

For a moment, he studied her, eyeing her perfectly formed features, her creamy, smooth skin. Though she looked like an ice princess now, he couldn't help but remember her in his arms. In the throes of passion, she'd looked blazingly, thrillingly alive. He had a fierce ache to see her that way again.

"What?" Glaring back at him, she brought one hand up to her face, a curiously self-conscious and human gesture. "Do I have something on my face, or what?"

"Just thinking." Though he wanted to touch her, he kept his hands clenched at his side.

"We've got to track them. To do that better, I need to change."

"Why?" She gave him a bleak look. "You know as well as I do that they didn't go on foot."

"Can Dani shape-shift yet?"

She froze. He could have sworn a look of guilt crossed her face as her frown deepened. "Yes. But she wouldn't have—"

"You never know. In the middle of the chaos, she may have changed while Addie fought them, and taken off. In her wolf shape, she could outrun any human."

For the first time since they'd arrived, hope lit her perfect features. "I didn't think of that. She could be free. By all means, change."

Might as well tell her all of it. He took a

deep breath. "Plus, when I'm wolf, I'll be able to identify the blood, whether it's Addie's or…"

Baring her fangs at the thought of her daughter bleeding, Marika nodded. "Do it. Now."

In a few swift motions, he stripped off his clothes. Removing his jewelry took a second more, and he placed that on top of his shirt. Then, dropping to all fours, he closed his eyes and began the change to wolf.

All the while, even when the change rippled through him, he was overwhelmingly conscious of her watching him. Even as his nose lengthened and fur appeared where once had been human skin, when he opened his eyes as wolf, her delicate features were the first thing he saw.

Marika. The woman he'd once believed was his mate.

As his other self, he padded toward the well-worn sweater draped over the back of the desk chair. Inhaling deeply, he got a flood of scent, immediately bringing to mind a rounded, older woman, with steely gray hair and sparkling blue eyes. *Addie*.

Then, he moved to the blood. Again, Addie. Relentless, he searched for other scents. The small cot finally yielded another, a familiar mixture of human and beast. Halfling shifter. Female. Young. This must be Dani.

He scoured the room with his nose, trying to locate another scent. He found none. If she'd walked away from her bed on her own two feet, she would have left traces of her scent on the floor. Their absence told him whoever had come here had snatched her up from the cot, giving her no chance to escape or change. Though they might have used chloroform to knock her out, at least he could venture a guess that she hadn't been seriously harmed.

Finally, knowing he could learn nothing else as wolf, he moved over to the spot where he'd left his clothes and began the change back to man.

Once completed, he turned his back to Marika while he dressed. As usual, when he returned to human form, he was fully aroused. Though clearly inappropriate, this was something he had no control over. Still, he didn't want her to see this aspect of him, not now.

All the while, she waited, a silent, perfect statue.

Only when he'd finished, did she move.

"Well?" she demanded. "What did you find out? Whose blood is it?"

"Addie's. She's the one who was hurt. She must have fought to protect Dani. The only trace of Dani's scent comes from her bed. They must have snatched her while she slept and used something to knock her out."

Their gazes locked. Held. Finally, seeing the abject terror in her eyes, Beck looked away, clenching his fists.

"I'm sorry," he said softly, aware that this was the only comfort he could allow himself to offer her now. "But I think they carried Dani out to their vehicle."

To distract himself, he went to the desk and, using a thick, black marker, scrawled the words Closed Until Further Notice on a piece of paper, which he then taped to the inside of the front window.

Finally, she stirred. Her determined expression made her look fierce. "What now?"

"Now, we've got to clean up this place. I also want to call Simon again. I think he can help put out feelers, see if we can at least get some sort of ID on who these people are. I'll have to leave a message, but he'll call me back as soon as he's able."

She nodded. "Thank you," she said.

Seeing the vulnerability in her face, he managed a curt nod and began straightening the furniture. After a moment, she moved quickly to help him, rolling up the bloody rug and stashing it in the utility closet.

"Without taking the time to paint, we can't do much about the bloodstained walls. I found this." She held up a large Bud Light poster. "I was thinking I could tack this up over the worst spot."

Watching her, it hit him again. "Addie," he said slowly. "For their sakes, Addie had better not be seriously hurt."

"I agree." Expression fierce, she looked every inch the Vampire Huntress. "Either way, they've hurt her. For that, they'll pay with their lives. Shifter or no, regardless of Pack law. Do you understand me?"

"Of course. I completely agree. This is personal."

A slow smile spread over her face. She touched his arm. "There's hope for you yet, Anton Beck."

"I don't know whether to take that as a compliment or an insult." The instant he spoke, her smile faded, making him regret his words.

"Let's get out of here," he said brusquely. "Even though we won't know where they went, I'll feel better hitting the road."

She shook her head, frowning again. "Look, I agreed to let you come here with me, but that's as far as we go together. From now on, I go alone." As she started for the door, his cell phone rang, stopping her in her tracks.

Slowly she turned, eyeing him.

Flashing her a look of satisfaction, Beck answered it. "Hello?"

"Anton Beck?" The unfamiliar female voice sounded ancient and imperious all at once.

Cautiously, he responded. "Yes."

"I am Brigid."

Marika's Priestess. "I've heard of you."

She continued as if he hadn't spoken. "I am the leader of the Vampire Huntresses. You may have heard of us."

She waited a beat for his assent, then continued. "As you're aware, Marika's child has been abducted. We are mobilizing forces to deal with this. Shifter, you leave her alone."

Statement, not question.

"Like hell I will. Dani's my daughter, too."

"You're a danger to her."

He would have found her statement laughable, if she hadn't sounded so serious.

"You're a fool if you think that."

She hissed, then made a sound like a low growl. "Think well before you defy me."

"I would never hurt my daughter." He let his certainty ring in his voice. Then he remembered something Marika had said earlier. "You told her I would, didn't you? You told Marika I was a danger to Dani."

Brigid spat her reply. "You're an idiot."

"Maybe." He took small satisfaction knowing he'd succeeded in rattling her. Getting the truth was far more important. "You didn't answer my question."

"Shifter, I do not need to tell you that this is of utmost importance. Let me speak to Marika."

"She's gone," he said, without bothering to look and see if that was indeed the truth.

"She's standing right behind you." Brigid's voice was silky smooth laced with steel. "Put her on."

A strong compulsion settled over him, urging him to immediately turn and do as she ordered. While he fought this, Marika snatched the phone out of his hands.

Furious, he let her. A cloud of foreboding settled over him. He recognized strong magic when he felt it. Did all vampires possess such magic, or was this because Brigid was High Priestess?

He made a mental note to ask Marika later. That is, if she stuck around long enough for him to ask anything. At least now he understood why she'd kept their daughter hidden from him and why she was so eager to ditch him now.

Turning, he eyed her. Since taking the phone from him, she'd barely uttered more than two syllables. Even now she stared blankly at nothing with narrowed eyes.

He wondered what vitriolic nonsense the old lady was spewing at her.

After a few minutes had passed, she murmured something that sounded like assent and closed the phone. Her expression told him nothing as she passed it back to him.

"What did she say?"

"More woo-woo bullshit. I'm tired of this."

"Why does she hate me?"

"She doesn't." Her automatic reply contained no conviction.

He stared, he couldn't help it. "What the hell do you mean? She actually believes I'd harm my daughter."

"She has visions. They usually come true."

"And she claims to have seen me harming Dani?"

"Not you specifically. A shifter."

"Of which there are millions. I don't believe this. Two years of my daughter's life, gone. All because of some old lady and her generic prophecy."

She bit her lip. "I couldn't take a chance. I had to protect my child."

"Our child."

"You've got to understand. Brigid can supposedly tell the future."

"Supposedly." He pounced on the word. "Do you doubt her?"

"Maybe I do, now. I don't know." Anger colored her voice. "If she can really see the future, why didn't she know they'd capture me and take Dani? If she has true visions, she should have already known. She could have prevented this."

The agony in her voice mirrored his own, amplifying it. Again, despite what she'd done, he ached to take her into his arms. Instead, he forced himself to concentrate on the matter at hand. "Does she know where Dani is now?"

"No. That's the thing. All my life, I've looked up to her. Her prophecies come true, always. She's the Vampire Seer, for plasma's sake. But if she's so damn powerful, why doesn't she know where they've taken Dani? I'm beginning to doubt her all-fired abilities."

"She has something," he felt compelled to point out. "I felt her magic."

"Really?" Shoving her hand through her hair, Marika's anger radiated from her. "I didn't. She's a powerful vampire witch. She's one of the oldest of my kind, reputedly ancient, a thousand years old or more."

He filed this information away for future reference. "What did she want?"

"To give me orders." Her voice dropped into a growl, eerily wolflike.

"She tried to give me orders, too. Are you going to follow them?"

Her frown deepened. "No vampire, Huntress or not, is allowed to refuse her orders."

"Answer the question." He felt a glimmer of hope. "Are you going to do what she asked?"

Finally, she met his gaze, her own remarkably clear and direct. "Some of it. Probably not all. She wanted me to ditch you."

Careful not to show any emotion, he nodded. "I'm not surprised."

"Yes, well, I'm beginning to think things aren't as black and white as she makes them sound."

He caught his breath, but said nothing.

"However," she continued, "if I ignore her completely, she'll probably send others to hunt me down and kill me."

"We'll deal with that when and if it happens. What do you want to do, Marika?"

She answered without hesitation. "Find Dani. And hunt and destroy the ones who took her. Brigid claims she can help me do that. After all, she has a stake in this, too."

This last comment surprised him. "What do you mean?"

"Brigid was supposed to begin training Dani,

once she turned five. This is a great honor among my people. I myself trained with her."

He felt a moment of grief. Had she been raised among his people, Dani would already have begun instruction in Pack heritage. He said nothing, aware that Marika wasn't ready to hear such a thing.

She squared her shoulders, lifting her chin and effectively wiping all emotion from her face. "Brigid told me something about herself. She says she's like Dani. Mixed. She claims she herself is the product of a union between an elf and a vampire."

Shocked despite himself, Beck scratched his head. "An elf? They can't have children, either. How would such a thing be possible?"

"Who knows?" She began to pace, agitated. "A few years ago I wouldn't have thought a shifter could impregnate me."

"True." He sensed there was more she wanted to tell him, only she couldn't find the words.

Blazing past him, she spun and went in the other direction, her long hair flying behind her. "But in Brigid's case, that would explain why she has such powerful magic. She got it from her elfin father."

"Is she actually a vampire then, or elf?"

"Both, I guess." She shrugged. "Like Dani."

"But you said Dani is alive."

"She is. Her heart beats, her lungs breathe. She's not dead like me."

"So it follows if Brigid was born of a vampire and is part elf, wouldn't she, too, be alive?"

"She's not." She spoke with certainty. "Like I said, she's over a thousand years old."

"Aren't elves immortal?"

An expression of surprise crossed her face. "I never thought of that."

"Or maybe she was born an elf and then was turned."

"Again, entirely possible. I know Brigid married another vampire, one even older than her. A vamp from ancient Egyptian times. Maybe he's the one who turned her."

He swore. "You guys have an even more messed-up history than we shifters do."

"We've been around longer." Abruptly reversing direction, she started for the door. "Are you ready?" she asked, her eyes blazing amber sparks at him.

Again, he felt a tug of attraction. Somehow, he kept his voice calm. "Are you saying you trust me now?"

"I'm going to do part of what Brigid asked. I'm ready to hit the road," she said. "With you."

Inhaling deeply, he managed a nonchalant nod. "Not enough of an answer. I need to know if you trust me."

"Look, Beck—"

"Answer the question."

"I barely know you anymore. It's been three years."

"You're still trying to avoid answering. If Brigid hadn't said a shifter would harm Dani, would you trust me?"

"I don't know. Dani was conceived the night Juliet was murdered."

Heart thumping steadily in his chest, he stared at her cold, exquisite face and waited for more.

She stared back, expression unreadable.

Finally, he nodded. "And?"

"Do you blame her for your sister's death?"

He saw from her tortured expression how much the admission cost her. Still, that she could even ask such a thing felt like a slap in the face. "How could you think that? She had nothing to do with what happened to Jules."

"No, but we did. She was waiting for us in the bar when the fight broke out. If we hadn't been making love, conceiving Dani, we would have been there, kept her from getting hurt."

How many times had he wondered the same thing himself? "You just said yourself, there are no guarantees. We could have been sitting right next to her and she might have still died."

Her chin came up. "I heard you thought the silver bullet was meant for you."

"Addie told you that?"

She nodded. "Yes. Yet earlier, when I mentioned the possibility that Jules was murdered, you didn't say anything."

"There didn't seem to be a point." He sighed. No mercy for the wicked. "Think about it. Those men had more reason to want me dead. I was a Protector. Or, alternatively, they could have killed her deliberately to hurt me. I might have eliminated one of their relatives. But I don't know. I'll never know now."

"Life's like that," she said sadly. "Sometimes we don't ever get answers."

"Back to your question. If anyone was responsible for Juliet's death, I was. And even then, I don't know that for a fact. Sometimes I think that's how I'm able to go on. Our daughter's conception was a gift in the face of a horrible tragedy. I only wish I'd been there to share it."

"From what I hear, you were in no condition to share anything."

Swallowing, he nodded. "Brutally honest, aren't you?"

"Yes. And if we're going to do this together, I expect the same from you."

Their gazes locked, held. Finally, he nodded. "Fine. Then you must have decided to trust me, at least a little."

"A little." Her concession came with a smile that vanished like a ghost. "You'll have to prove yourself to me."

"I can do that."

"Good. And, Beck? The second I feel even the slightest threat toward Dani, I'll kill you myself. Consider this fair warning."

At least she always spoke her mind; he'd give her that. Despite everything, despite her taking their daughter and vanishing from his life, despite her threat, every time he glanced at her, he felt attraction like a punch to the gut.

He'd always known Marika was resilient, but he'd never realized how strong she was. She'd kept their daughter safe, at great personal cost to herself. Her strength matched her extraordinary beauty.

He'd accept her challenge. "Heard and acknowledged. Are you going to tell me what Brigid asked?"

"Yes, eventually." She considered him for a moment. "There's something else you need to know as well, but I'll tell you once we get going."

"Where do you want to go?"

"Where Brigid told me to." Tossing her hair across her shoulder, she yanked open the door. "I don't know why, but for some reason, I'm not entirely sure I should trust her."

"Then why go where she tells you to?"

"Well, if we're moving, at least I feel like we're doing something."

He nodded. "What's she going to do once she finds out I'm with you?"

"I have no idea. I'm not going to worry about

that now. We'll figure out the rest once we're in the truck."

And she disappeared outside, leaving him no choice but to follow.

Chapter 5

Striding toward the truck, Marika wondered if Beck realized how much her decision to trust him cost her. It had been so long since she'd trusted anyone except Addie. Opening herself up, even a small crack, made her feel naked and exposed.

He'd asked for her trust, but he'd said nothing about reciprocating. She couldn't blame him for that. She certainly hadn't given him reason to trust her. After all, she'd kept their daughter from him for the entire two years of Dani's life.

His pain and sense of loss had been deep,

she could tell. So had his shock and anger upon learning he had a two-year-old child he'd never met. He wouldn't easily forgive what could only be regarded as a betrayal. Men like Beck, who lived by a code of honor set so much higher than others, would find it hard to understand her reasons for doing what she'd done.

Climbing in the truck beside her, Beck didn't speak as he fitted the key in the ignition and fired up the engine. Carefully, she avoided looking at him, wondering if he knew how much she'd missed him. She'd spent many a sleepless night, tossing and turning, wondering if she'd done the right thing by keeping their child a secret from him. Despite Brigid's warnings, a part of her had always doubted and wondered.

And now she wondered, too, how he'd react when he learned the rest of the truth about their daughter. He'd claimed to want to know Dani, to love her. Would this change once he learned what she was?

She sighed, wishing she could settle her jittery nerves. She needed to think clearly in this, the worst crisis she'd ever faced. Awful enough that her daughter—their daughter—was missing.

Worse that every time their gazes met, desire slammed into her, as strong as it had been three years ago. Even now, when she was crazy with worry over their daughter. Every time she looked at him, with his mussed spiked black hair, torn jeans and soulful amber eyes, she wanted him.

Losing her baby girl, knowing her own child was in danger, made her desire more than inappropriate. Her mouth twisted. She needed to focus on finding Dani rather than lusting over Dani's father. Look what had happened last time she'd given in—her best friend, Juliet, Beck's sister—had been murdered.

Sneaking a glance at his profile, she steeled herself against her belly-deep reaction. Though he was obviously concentrating intensely on the road, when he felt her gaze on him, he shot her a look cautiously laced with curiosity.

"Where to?" he asked. "Or are we planning to aimlessly drive the roads? We can head down to Presidio and the Border, or go west to El Paso. And there's always Alpine and Marfa. Any idea where we should look?"

Instantly, she shook her head. "I don't know. I have absolutely no idea where they've taken her. We need to head toward the mountains. There's a house there. That's all she said." Brigid really should have given her more information.

She hated operating so blind. Especially when finding Dani was so important. Inside her head, Marika could hear an invisible clock ticking, reminding her that they were running out of time.

Dani was missing. Her disappearance was made worse by the fact that her mother felt completely and utterly helpless. She, a Master Huntress, with her fangs clipped. It took every ounce of self-control to keep from giving in to blind panic. Maybe this obsession with Beck was her subconscious's way of distraction.

"We've got to find Dani."

"I know," he said, his voice calmly reassuring. "We will. Let's start asking around in town. That'd be a good starting point. I promise you, we will find her."

Whether he honestly believed that or not, she couldn't tell. She couldn't afford not to believe it. Without that hope to cling to, she'd simply go insane.

For a woman who'd spent the past hundred-odd years in action, this aimless wandering felt wrong. Asking around in town would be a start, but even that didn't seem to be enough. She had to do *something more*. Anything. But what? Patience had never been her strong suit. Nor Beck's, if she remembered right.

Shifters had Dani, she just knew it.

The big question—could she trust Beck to help, even if doing so meant he had to go against his own kind? He'd been a Protector, a member of an elite Pack Society sworn to protect shape-shifters. How would that loyalty balance against whatever feelings he might have for her and the child they'd created together?

"There was more to Brigid's warning," she began.

"You mean the one where she warned you against me?" His tone held layers of mockery and pain.

"Yes."

"Well?" he finally asked, hands on the steering wheel. "Are you going to tell me?"

Her stomach twisted. Ah, the moment of

truth. She'd have to be very careful when she judged his response. Would she be able to tell if he lied?

She had to hope she would. She didn't have the energy to play games with him. Not now, not in the midst of crisis. If she registered the slightest bit of hesitation on his part, then he would have to leave. Or she would have to escape him.

Glancing at her sideways, he frowned. "What's up with you? From what I remember, you've never had a problem with speaking your mind before."

"True." But so much was riding on his reaction. She took one deep breath, trying to regain her equilibrium.

They'd reached the end of the rutted road, coasting to a gravelly stop at the highway. Beck watched her, waiting. "Left or right? Marfa or Alpine? Where do you want to search first?"

Taking another deep breath, she chose and pointed east, toward the rising sun. "That way."

He gave one final glance in her direction. "Are you okay in sunlight?"

"Of course."

"You sound so certain," he mused. "Yet I've

always heard most vamps have to hide in the darkness."

"That's fairy-tale stuff. Only the newly made have to hide in darkness." She had the most absurd urge to chew her nails, a habit she'd kicked centuries ago. This was ridiculous. She barely recognized herself. For over a hundred years, right up until Dani's birth, she'd been a Huntress, one of the fiercest of the fierce. Others of her kind respected and feared her. She'd been invincible. She needed to draw on that strength now.

"Once I say what I have to say, I'll need to ask you a question. I need complete honesty from you."

"Understood." Another sharp glance. Impatience colored his voice. "Now will you get on with it? Tell me the rest of what Brigid said."

"You're not going to like it any more than I do."

"Quit stalling."

"Fine." She lifted her chin. "Even before Dani was born, Brigid said the danger would come from the Pack."

"From Pack?" The sharp tone of his voice

matched the cutting look he gave her. "Pack in general, or just me?"

"Both. Before Dani was even born, she saw a vision. She warned me to avoid any and all shape-shifters. Including you. And now, her vision has proved true. Your people were the ones who kidnapped her. Shape-shifters have Dani."

He made no sound. She studied him, worried, but couldn't read his grim-faced expression. If she'd shocked him, he didn't show it.

"And you have proof of this how?"

"I don't need proof. Brigid told me in detail what would happen. She wanted me to stay with her, under her protection, for that very reason. She *saw* the Pack kidnap Dani. She didn't know if you were behind it or if the threat came from others."

Jaw tight, he continued to drive. When he finally spoke, he asked a question. "She doesn't know why?"

"No. Now for the big question." Letting a mocking note creep into her voice since she was wary of his answer, she turned in her seat to face him. "So, Protector. To rescue Dani, you will have to go against your own kind. Are you prepared to do that?"

"Of course." He didn't even hesitate. "I've gone against my own before. If those shifters mean to harm our little girl, I'll kill them myself."

She felt a prickle of pleasure at the way he phrased his declaration and then ruthlessly squashed it. "*If?* Why else would they have taken her, if not to harm her?"

"I don't know. I think she might be too valuable to harm. Didn't your priestess tell you that?"

She rubbed the back of her neck. The pulsing knot there spoke of her frustration. "No. She doesn't know."

"It makes no sense." He sounded grim. "Dani is Pack and we protect our own. Why would shifters have done this?"

"Maybe they don't want her raised by a vampire."

"You're her mother. Who better to raise her?"

Though he'd intuitively known Dani was valuable, he didn't know the rest of it—what Dani was, what she could become. More than just an ordinary shape-shifter. Still trying to figure out how to tell him, she settled back in her seat and turned her head, giving herself time to think.

The brightening sunlight glared on the flat landscape, making heat spirals off in the distance. She always loved far-west Texas. The primitive surroundings had a stark kind of beauty, savage and simple, which suited her. She'd felt at home here—or had, until her daughter had been taken from her.

Now she felt like the proverbial fish out of water.

Even if Brigid had told her she was close to finding her, she wasn't certain she believed her. And Brigid's plan? Would it truly work?

He touched her shoulder, making her jump. "Marika, I know there's more."

"Don't touch me." She had to bite the side of her cheek to keep from lashing out at him.

Narrow-eyed, he stared. A muscle worked in his jaw. "Why not? Do you honestly believe I'd hurt a child, my own daughter?"

"No. That's not it."

"Then why?"

"I'm angry with myself." She spat the words.

"Look at me, what I am, what I can do. Yet I failed to protect a helpless two-year-old. What does that make me?"

"What did Brigid want you to do?"

She ignored his question, repeating her own. "I asked you, what does that make me?"

"A mother who's nearly out of her mind with worry."

All at once, all the fury went out of her, and she sagged against the seat. "I've been a Huntress for a couple hundred years, yet I never knew fear until I held my baby girl in my arms. I'm trying not to panic. Do you realize how much I want my daughter? I need my daughter, now. Every instinct inside me screams that I need to *do something,* but what? I'm powerless, in the dark. I don't know where she is or why they've taken her."

"Your priestess has her magic. She claims to have visions. Do you think she knows more than she's telling you?"

"She claims not to. But I'll tell you this." She took a deep breath, forcing herself to remain relatively calm. "If Brigid, the almighty Vampire Priestess, knows something that will help me find Dani, then I'll do whatever she asks. That's why we're going where she asks us to."

He digested this in silence. Then he asked, "And if she's wrong?"

"Brigid is never wrong. Or so they say. But if I learn she's only playing me for some obscure reason of her own, then neither heaven nor hell can help her. I'll hunt her down myself and make her pay."

He flashed her a quick smile. "There's my Vampire Huntress."

She wasn't his anything.

"One thing occurs to me," he continued. "What if the shifters took Dani to protect her from Brigid?"

Once, such a statement would have infuriated her. Now, she didn't even flinch. "I've already considered every possibility, including this one, and discarded it. Why would they do that? Brigid wouldn't harm her."

"Are you certain?" He sounded skeptical.

"Not one hundred percent. You know as well as I do that anything's possible. Look at what happened in your Society."

He raised one brow. "You heard about that?"

One of the leaders of the Society of Protectors had tried to form his own organization, using cloned shifters to create the prefect Protector. He'd planned to brainwash them and make them answerable only to him and had exterminated anyone who'd gotten in his way.

"Everyone heard about that. It was used as an example among the Huntresses as what can happen with too much power."

"Yet you seem to believe Brigid when she says it's Pack that stole Dani."

"She has no reason to lie."

He continued to stare at her, skepticism plain in his face. "You think not? That's what I thought, when things started going wrong at the Society. I dared to question them, and for that, I was almost killed."

"That was you?"

"I was one of many who rebelled and fought back. My friend Simon tried to save a female Feral from extermination. Turned out she was his mate."

"A Feral? Like a wild shifter?"

"We have them. More than you know. One of our duties as Protectors was to save and rehabilitate them. The ones who were too far gone, too mad, or were a danger to themselves and others, had to be exterminated. It got so bad we had a virtual standing order to kill them on sight."

"Wow." She bit her lip. "Now I understand why you quit."

"Yeah. So my point is, don't rush to judgment. If shifters took Dani, they may have had good reason."

She didn't want to hear such nonsense. "They have no right. How can you even say such a thing, knowing they attacked so violently? Dani is mine."

To give him credit, he didn't continue to press his case. Probably because he knew he didn't have one. Instead, he simply drove as she directed, asking no questions. She let the sound of the engine and the uneven pavement under the tires soothe her frazzled nerves somewhat.

Finally, she felt she could speak calmly enough to tell him the rest of it. "Brigid is sending others to help me—us. That's where we're heading."

"Reinforcements? Vampires, I assume?"

"I guess." She knew she didn't sound happy. "She said they would fill me in when I met up with them. I've gotta tell you, though, I've never been much of a team player."

"Me, either." Grim-voiced, he looked as unhappy as she felt. "I mean, I had to when I was a Protector, but that's one of the reasons I left. Things get out of hand too easily when a mob gets together."

"Yeah. I agree. But once again, until I have a reason not to, I've got to do what Brigid asks, so we're meeting up with them in a house in the mountains."

"Where?"

She rattled off the address from memory. "I've been there once or twice over the years. The vampire who owns it is on an extended vacation in Europe."

Beck frowned. "That address sounds familiar." Keeping one hand on the wheel, he rummaged in his pocket, pulling out a crumpled piece of paper and squinting at it. "Yep. That's the same place I've rented for the next six months."

She stared, incredulous. "You rented a vampire's house?"

"Give me a break. I didn't know who owned it."

"Doesn't that bother you?"

"No. Should it?" Grimacing, he shot her a disgusted look. "I can't say I really care, as long as it's nice."

"You don't know?"

"No. I haven't even been by there yet. Addie's the one who set this up. I was going to pick up my keys from her."

Again, he'd managed to shock her. "Addie set this up?"

"Yeah." He shot her a glance. "I don't understand. Why is this so weird to you?"

"Let's see. This entire thing has been nothing but a nightmare. First, someone grabbed me and drugged me. Then you show up, captured by the same people."

"And now they've got our daughter."

"And now they've got my daughter. Oh, and then you tell me you're renting a house in the middle of a vampire enclave. What's next?" She couldn't keep the agitation from her voice. "A vampire-shifter war? Addie knows better. She might be human, but she's always been incredibly savvy about this kind of stuff."

"What kind of stuff? You're not making sense." Beck sounded genuinely confused.

"Who cares where I rent a house? A war? Why would you even say such a thing?"

"Because a shifter renting Vlad's house would be like lighting a match to gunpowder."

"Aren't you being a bit dramatic? Things aren't that fragile. The truce between vamps and shifters has been in place for at least ten years."

"The truce has always been shaky. And ten years is nothing to a vampire. Let me give you an example. Four years ago, when Juliet and I visited here for one of Vlad's famous parties, several of the older vamps got upset that a shifter dared to enter their territory. I had to do a lot of fancy politicking to calm them down. Vlad finally asked us to leave."

Beck shook his head. "Are you kidding me?"

"No."

"For God's sake, this is the twenty-first century."

"I know and you know that, but we're talking about vampires that are centuries old. They barely give lip service to the truce. I've heard only Brigid's power keeps them reined in."

Rubbing the back of his neck, he swallowed hard. "This is completely unbelievable. But since you promised not to lie to me, I have to accept that it's true. Which makes it even worse that Brigid wants you to go there. How do you think her vampire helpers are going to react to me? Won't they have a problem with me being a shifter?"

"Probably. But then again, they've been handpicked by Brigid, so I don't know. Maybe that's why she's gotten involved in all this. Usually, she doesn't pay much attention to the goings-on of lesser beings."

"I see."

She gave him a curious look. "What will you do if they do have a problem with you?"

"I don't want to start a war. Most importantly, I don't want to do anything that would cause a delay in getting Dani back."

Despite herself, his words touched her. "Thanks for that. I wonder if Brigid knows yet that I'm bringing you with me. She must know."

"What does she have to gain by playing games?"

"And endangering the life of my child." She finished what he did not.

"Exactly."

She wondered how they could think so alike. After all, they came from completely different backgrounds. "I hope, once her minions get here, they'll fill us in on what exactly is going on. This delay—any delay—is killing me. I need to find my baby and make sure she's safe."

Beck didn't respond. She glanced his way to find him intent on the road ahead, the clean lines of his chiseled profile, so eerily familiar, again caught her by surprise.

Mate. The word whispered in her soul, horrifying her. Dani resembled her father so much, looking at him made her chest hurt.

Suddenly she wondered if it would be easier with him out of the picture. "You don't have to do this, you know."

Now he turned to look at her, his gaze blank. "What do you mean?"

"I mean you have a choice. I don't know what Brigid has planned, who she's sending to help us. This could be dangerous for you. You can still walk away."

A muscle worked in his jaw. "Marika, do you honestly think I'd abandon my own child because I was worried about my safety?" His voice rose. "What kind of an ass do you take me for?"

She had to smile. Then, inexplicably, her throat closed, and her eyes filled with tears.

Beck only saw the smile. "You seriously find this amusing?" Fury simmered in his voice. He stomped hard on the accelerator, sending the truck fishtailing. Tight-lipped, he said nothing else as they barreled down the road, heading into the rising sun.

She tried to speak, but knew if she did, she'd only start weeping. Ruthlessly, she tried to get herself under control. She spent a few seconds bucking herself up before she could turn her head and face him.

Opening her mouth, she began to explain, but he cut her off before she could get out a single word.

"You know, sometimes I wonder if you knew me at all...." His voice trailed off.

This got her attention. "What do you mean?"

Glancing at her, the hard lines of his jaw seemed to soften. "My sister loved you so much." When he swallowed, she couldn't help but follow the line of his masculine throat. "I miss her."

"I do, too." She awkwardly tried to comfort him, though she couldn't bring herself to actually touch him. "I loved her, too."

"After she died, every breath I took felt like it seared my lungs. The guilt was tremendous."

This was what she'd meant when she'd asked him if he hated Dani. She felt as if she had rocks in her mouth. "How did you manage to go on?"

"I ran in place." He gave her a quick, humorless smile. "You always hear the phrase take it day by day, you know? But there's some truth in that, though in my case I took it minute by minute, hour by hour. I told myself, if I could just make it until noon, until one, until five, I'd be okay. Every single day, I lived like that. And somehow, the sun kept rising and setting, the world moved on. I existed and learned to bury my pain."

While she'd had her pregnancy to distract her. "You're brave, you know."

"Not really." He waved her away. "You lost your best friend, too."

"I had my little girl. If anything happens to her…"

"Your Priestess would have told you if Dani was in immediate danger, would she not?"

"I don't know." She knew she sounded flat. "I don't know what she saw or didn't see. She wasn't exactly forthcoming with details."

"Something's got to give."

"You think?" Raw sarcasm mingled with the anger. "If Brigid has even the faintest inkling of where they've taken my daughter, she'd sure as hell better share it."

"I'm sure she will. Why else would she bother sending reinforcements?"

"That's another thing I don't get. Why does Brigid think we *need* reinforcements? I'm a Vampire Huntress, you're a Pack Protector. We're two elite members of our species. Surely the two of us can handle a couple of ordinary kidnappers, even if they are shifters."

"Maybe they're not ordinary."

She made a rude sound. "All I know is Brigid's people had better be waiting when we get there. Otherwise, they can try to catch up with us."

"We don't know where to look."

"True. A major sticking point. Without Brigid, we could go running off in a thousand wrong directions. Maybe you should try your Protector friends again. They have the technology to help us locate her."

"They'll call me when they're ready."

"I'll give them another half hour, then I'll call them myself. Look, there." She pointed ahead, where the road undulated down a hill and across a flat expanse of land. "Turn left once we cross that valley."

"Toward the mesa?"

"Yep. Vlad's house is on the incline."

She wasn't kidding. The house, stucco and glass and weathered cedar, perched halfway up the mesa as though a hardscrabble climb had gained it a foothold there. The morning sun reflected off the wall of windows, sending bright pinpricks of light back out into the rising heat of the day.

As they pulled up in the driveway, the garage door began to rise.

Startled, Beck looked at Marika. "Do you have an opener?"

She shook her head. "No. But look, they obviously do."

Three vampires stood in the empty garage, so still they might have been made of stone, waiting.

Chapter 6

Brigid's reinforcements. Hellhounds. Beck let the truck coast to a stop and killed the ignition. The vampires hadn't moved.

He glanced at Marika. "Do you know them?"

"One of them looks familiar. The woman, though I don't know where I've seen her." She didn't sound happy. "The other two, I don't recognize. But they're old, all of them. Ancient."

And now coming toward them. Like most of their kind, the vampires moved effortlessly, with an otherworldly sort of grace. Their perfect skin glowed pearly white in the bright sun.

The two males were tall and slender, wearing dark suits that were both well-fitting and expensively made. With their well-groomed hair and chiseled features, they looked savagely elegant. In direct contrast, the female appeared exquisitely deadly in her curve-hugging, black spandex jumpsuit and five-inch stiletto heels.

Together, they looked like denizens from a chic version of hell. Dangerous messengers.

A shiver ran up the back of his spine, instinctual reaction to a centuries-old nemesis. Until the treaty, his kind had hunted them, battled them and sought their death. They'd been sworn enemies, vamps and shifters, and to this day much of the distrust remained on both sides.

The three vampires glided to a stop a short distance from the truck, waiting for them to emerge. Again, Beck felt a premonition of danger. While he'd never feared bloodsuckers before, these weren't your everyday, run-of-the-mill vampires. His first instinct—and one he trusted implicitly—was to recoil in repugnance.

A quick glance at Marika told him nothing; her nonexpression might have been chiseled from the same perfect stone as the other three vamps.

"Now what?" he asked.

Careful to avoid meeting his gaze, she shrugged and pushed open her door. "We find out what they know."

He jumped down, too, conscious that his wolf had become completely alert. The hair on his arms rose as if from static electricity. Moving toward them, he schooled his expression to match Marika's.

As they drew near, the two men kept their gazes riveted on Marika. The vampire woman watched Beck.

"You brought a pet with you?" she purred to Marika, the slight tilt at the corner of her eyes giving her an exotic appearance.

"Not a pet. An ally. Surely Brigid told you of him?"

"Perhaps she did. No matter." The woman dipped her chin, slanting Beck a mocking smile. "I am Renenet. You can call me Renee."

Marika's eyes widened. "Goddess of Fortune?"

"So I've been called." She lifted one shoulder in an elegant and disaffected shrug. "I am an old friend of Brigid, from the times before."

Which meant that this one was very, very old. Also very powerful.

"This is Heh." Waving her hand languidly, she indicated the tallest of the two men. "And finally, Usi."

Beck had to ask. "What do their names mean?"

When she turned that glowing gaze on him again, this time he felt the strength of her power. More magic. How many of these vampires were witches?

"Heh is the God of Immeasurable and Usi means smoke."

Usi's mouth spread into a thin-lipped smile. "Smoke comes in handy sometimes."

"You were supposed to come alone." Renee turned her violet gaze on Marika. "Do you dare disobey Brigid?"

"I do what I have to. Enough of this. What do you know about my daughter?" Letting a rasp of anger color her voice, Marika eyed each of them in turn. "What has Brigid told you?"

Before anyone could answer, the wind began

to blow, gusting in fierce spurts, as though from the dying breath of an unseen cyclone.

Beck spread his legs for balance and braced himself against the forceful air. Beside him, Marika did the same. The three others, without appearing to move, glided back into the shelter of the garage, eyes glowing in the dim space.

They did not invite Beck and Marika to join them.

And the wind continued to buffet them. Beck's sense of unease increased. Fleetingly, he wondered if even nature was trying to warn them.

"This is ridiculous," Marika shouted, glaring at the vamps. "Invite us in."

Surprised, Beck glanced from her to their hosts. Was that old bit of folklore actually true? Vamps couldn't go inside a residence unless invited? Hmm. He'd file that away for future reference and ask Marika about it.

Finally, he took Marika's arm and led her into the garage and out of the increasingly powerful air. Once inside, she shook him off and stalked to one side, keeping a distance between her and everyone else.

No one spoke. The three vamps continued to stare, as expressionless as statues.

"A storm is coming," Beck finally said, uncomfortable with the silence. He could swear he heard a voice shrieking unintelligible words in cadence with the wind. A child's voice. A little girl. Dani?

Imagination. Had to be.

Usi's lips twitched. "Somewhere, the earth Goddess is angry," he commented, bestowing on them a faint smile. "I hear her rage in the wind's fury."

"Not the Goddess. Her child," the vampire woman said, turning her unsettlingly sharp-eyed focus on Marika. "Your daughter calls out to you. Can you not hear her screaming your name on the wind?"

He'd been right. Cocking his head, Beck listened. Now he could tell for certain. The gut-wrenching sound of his daughter crying for her mother. Fury and a toddler's anguish mingled in the air, making him want to lash out in a blind attempt to help her.

"She calls you," he said, taking care to hide his gut reaction from the others. Hearing his child's voice for the first time, in such a powerful way, nearly brought him to his knees. He could only imagine how this made Marika feel.

Meaning to offer comfort, however small, he touched Marika's shoulder. She shot him a look so full of anguish, he felt it like a knife.

"I don't…" She bit her lip.

"You cannot hear her?" Renee asked.

Slowly, Marika shook her head. Making no sound, she pushed away from the others, wrapping her arms around her middle, as though she'd been struck in the stomach. Lost in her own private grief, unable to find comfort.

Beck started for her, but the vampire called Heh materialized in front of him, blocking his path.

"Wait," the other growled. "You cannot help her with this."

Beck ignored him, shouldering him away. "Move."

For the space of a second, their gazes locked. Man and vampire—no, *wolf* and vampire. Once Beck let Heh see the wolf behind his eyes, the vamp conceded.

With an elegant shrug, Heh stepped back.

Marika closed her eyes, her face contorted with her misery.

The sound of Dani's need intensified, perhaps fueled by a connection with her mother's obvious pain.

"Marika." Beck wrapped her in his arms. Though her posture felt rigid and stiff, she didn't resist. She simply allowed his embrace. It was as though she'd simply vacated her body.

Still he held her, willing her to accept what little comfort he could give. He hated to see her so silent and defeated. Even anger would be better than this.

But she didn't move—not to sag against him, not to break her frozen despair. The silence stretched on, both awkward and painful in the face of the ever-present wind still carrying Dani's cries. In a way, he was glad Marika couldn't hear them because the heartbreaking sound brought a fiery need to do more.

When he finally stepped back, she gave him a broken, hard-edged look, full of grief.

"I can't hear her," she said, her voice echoing her agonized expression. "Yet you all can. Dani calls to me, her mother, but I don't recognize her voice. How can that be?" Her voice broke.

She glared at Renenet, as if she believed the older vampire responsible. "Why can't I hear my own daughter, while you—a total stranger—can?"

"I don't know. Perhaps you are not listening hard enough." Renee's harsh voice didn't soften.

"Too much worry and fear can cloud your abilities," Heh agreed. "Clear your mind and then try again."

"If you let her, she will reach you. Your girl is already very powerful," Renenet said.

With a nod, Marika closed her eyes and began taking deep breaths. She missed the hard glance the two male vampires exchanged. Beck shot them the same kind of look.

"What kind of creature *is* this child?" Usi snarled. "So small, yet she can send her voice out over the wind."

But Renenet now watched Beck. "You heard her, too, right?" she asked. "So this is not something only detected by vampires?"

"I'm her father," he said, even though doing so felt a bit like rubbing salt in Marika's open wound.

Now, he watched the play of emotion on Marika's perfect face as she strained yet again to hear Dani's plaintive cry. Meanwhile, he clung to the sound, even though doing so made his inner wolf want to howl. Keeping the beast under control proved a Herculean effort, occupying all his self-control, yet he refused to try to block out the sound of his daughter's voice. This, his first connection, no matter how painful, brought him hope. As long as they could hear her, that meant she was still alive.

The other three vampires exchanged glances. They all waited for Marika while she cocked her head and continued to try to hear. Their faces were too beautiful and so expressionless that they might have been carved from stone.

Unlike Marika, who looked as though she might shatter into a thousand pieces.

Finally, she made a sound of defeat and opened her eyes. "Nothing," she said, her gaze locking with Beck's.

Aching for her, still battling his wolf, he dipped his chin in acknowledgment.

She shifted her gaze to Heh, then to Renee. "You all heard her, didn't you? Everyone but me." Shadows darkened her eyes.

"Yes, this is true." Heh's perfect expression never changed. "Your child is very powerful. What kind of magic does she wield?"

"She's just a little girl." Marika glared at him, wiping her streaming eyes with the back of her hand. "She has no magic."

"Or perhaps it's well-hidden." Renenet moved restlessly, making a circle around the perimeter of the small garage. Beck noted that all the while, she managed not to turn her back on him.

Smart vampire.

"I want to hear her," Marika said, her voice troubled.

The other woman shook her head. "She has gone silent. If she cries again and you don't hear her, I will tell you to listen."

Beck could tell from her rigid posture that Marika didn't like this, but finally she dipped her head in acquiescence.

Once she had, Renenet stood still, as if satisfied.

Now Marika moved, watching her like a hawk. "Tell me what Brigid has told you about my daughter's capture. Do you know where she is?"

"We have been told that we must help you find your daughter. If we do not, Brigid has seen the beginning of a terrible war. When our people battle each other on such a scale, many lives will be lost. Not just us, but precious few humans would survive such a cataclysmic conflict."

"War?" Marika stared. "That's insane. What has any of this to do with me and my child?"

Renee's eyes gleamed. "Your little girl is... unique, is she not?

They all waited, the two male vamps appearing fascinated while Beck was confused. Of course Dani was unique. She was the child of a shifter and a vampire.

But for the space of a heartbeat, Marika looked...trapped. Fear, stark and vivid, filled her eyes. Then, so quickly a blink might have made him miss it, she again composed her features into that perfect mask.

"Dani is a two-year-old child who learned early to change form. There is no reason to think she would cause a war."

The other vamps didn't appear convinced.

"If she is harmed, you would seek to destroy those that have taken her, would you not?"

The sharp glance Marika sent his way told Beck her answer before she even spoke.

"You know what I would do. And I don't

think anyone here would dare to tell me I'd be wrong."

"They are shifters," Renee continued smoothly. "One vampire attack and the truce is off."

"They have already broken the truce by snatching my daughter," Marika responded sharply, appearing on the verge of abandoning all pretense.

"You see? Do you then advocate a war? Now, between us and all shifters?"

Again, Marika shot Beck a glance. "No. I'm not a fool. This is between me and the creeps who took Dani. Not all vampires and all shifters."

"But there is more," Usi put in. "Because of what your child is—"

"Enough." Cutting him off, Renee paced restlessly. "This talk leads to nothing."

Usi bared his fangs, his vampire mannerisms so similar to that of an angry shifter that Beck nearly spoke his thoughts out loud. Only the knowledge that the other man wouldn't appreciate such a comparison kept him silent.

"I would not be opposed to such a war," Heh said.

"Brigid would." Renee's sharp reprimand

left no room for a retort. "You will do as you promised and help find this powerful child."

"Dani." Marika sounded weary. "Her name is Dani. Though she's half shifter and half vampire, she's only a little girl. If she has magic, she doesn't know how to use it."

"And he really is the father?" Renee asked Marika.

"Yes."

"But only a mere shape-shifter. Interesting. The only other times a vampire has borne a child were only possible because the sire was an elf. We've always believed this was due to elvin magic."

Was this a test, confirming what they already knew? Marika sighed. "I don't know how it happened. I made love with a shifter, with him. The next thing I knew, I was pregnant."

"Does her heart beat?" Heh's voice was savage.

"Yes. Red blood flows through her veins, her heart beats and she breathes. She cannot go without sleeping, and she eats and drinks regular food, not blood. She's smart and funny and beautiful." Her voice cracked, but she continued. "And I love her.

"And though she's only two, she already can shape-shift," Marika said.

"Is this unusual among your kind?" Heh asked Beck.

Though he didn't trust them, Beck saw no reason not to answer. "Yes. Even in Halflings."

"Halflings?" Renee asked.

"Those of our kind who are not full-blooded shifters."

"She is not vampire." Renee spoke decisively. "I don't understand why Brigid believes she's so important."

"Obviously someone else does, too." Heh's dry tone matched his impassive face. "Someone kidnapped her, according to Brigid."

"What are you going to do about it?" Beck put in. The vampires ignored him.

With a savage smile, Beck continued. "I thought you were supposed to help us. We're running out of time. Dani's missing."

"And I want her back." Marika glanced from Heh to Beck, a pain-filled look of entreaty on her face. "You've got to help us."

"Do you help or hinder, Shifter?" Renee demanded, her hard-edged gaze cutting.

Beck stepped around her, moving to Marika's side. He took her hand firmly in his. "She is my daughter. Of course I help. But even more, Dani is Pack. We Pack protect our own."

"But according to Brigid, Pack are the ones who've taken her," Usi pointed out.

"Which makes no sense."

"Why not? Pack hate vampires. The child is half."

"No," Beck insisted. "We don't look at things that way. She is a Halfling, she can change, therefore she's Pack. There's no reason for anyone to wish her harm."

"Unless—" Renee dipped her head toward Marika "—there is something she's not telling us."

Beck fully expected Marika to deny this. After all, she'd promised to give him only the truth.

Instead, she straightened her shoulders and took a deep breath. "I can only assume Brigid already knows, right?"

"Knows what?" Beck wondered if he was the only one in the dark. "What is it you're not telling me?"

But Renee and her two cohorts waited, too,

watching Marika, who stiffened. Her very posture spoke of defiance.

"Dani can change shapes, it's true," she finally said. "But she can do more than the average shifter. She can become not only a wolf, but something else. Something like a...griffon. But instead of a lion's body, she's a wolf. A wolf with wings. She can fly, too." She shot a glance at Beck as she spoke.

All three of the vampires made sounds of shock. Stunned, Beck scarcely heard them.

"You didn't think this was important enough to tell me?" Anger choked him. "Your Dani is no mere Halfling. She's the stuff of legends. A being like this comes along only once in centuries."

"In a millennium," Renee corrected him, her dark eyes gleaming with what looked like excitement. "Dani is more than all of us."

"Does Brigid know this?" Usi asked.

Marika shook her head no.

"So we are searching for a god?" Usi looked unhappy with this possibility. "If she's so all-powerful, why can she not escape herself?"

"She's not a god. She's a small child." Hands

clenched in fists, Marika appeared ready to fight them all.

Beck didn't care. She'd already betrayed him. Again. "You promised me the truth," he reminded her. "And you lied."

"I didn't." Up came the chin. "I hadn't gotten around to telling you yet."

"Omission is a form of falsehood."

She froze, lowering her gaze to the floor. "I thought it would be easier if you didn't know."

"Easier how? You say shifters took her, but you didn't know why. For all you know, they are protecting Dani. Legend or no, she's as much a part of the Pack as she is a vampire."

Heh growled, again reminding Beck of a wolf. Odd that a vampire could have so many shifter traits. Glaring at him, Renenet immediately shushed him.

"Shifter, are you leaving us then?"

"I'm going nowhere." Crossing his arms, Beck waited for them to argue. "I will find my daughter, no matter what it takes."

As one, the three others turned their attention to Marika.

Again, thunder rumbled. Far off in the distant slate-gray horizon, lightening slashed the sky.

"A storm is coming." Marika's toneless voice spoke of her decision to say no more about her child's unique abilities. "If you hear my daughter again, I want to know what she says. Maybe she can tell us how to find her. In the meantime, tell me what Brigid has asked you to do."

"Asked *us* to do. The old ones are gathering in Greece." Renee sounded smug. "The full council."

Marika's sharp intake of breath was her only reply to this. From what Beck knew of vampires, a gathering of this magnitude meant things were dire indeed, or about to become that way.

Renee's exotic eyes found Beck's. "Shifter, Brigid asks that you alert the leaders of your Pack."

"Really?" Beck raised a brow. "I was supposed to be gone. When did she ask this?"

"Do you plan to quibble over small issues or find your daughter?" Her haughty voice irked him, but she was right.

"I will notify them. Dani's birth is an event of major significance."

Renee continued to focus on Beck. "Do you have a way to let them know?"

"I have a call in to one of my friends who's a Protector. He has connections. I'll let him know. He should be calling me back soon."

"Good. I think—"

"Don't." Marika stepped forward, interrupting the other woman. "You were sent here to help me. So don't act like you're taking over. I care nothing about meetings or gatherings. All I care about is Dani. I *will* find my daughter. Are you going to help me or not?"

Mouth tightening, Renee stared. Finally she nodded, leaning close. "We will do as Brigid asks," she said loudly, as though someone else could hear them. In a whisper, she spoke again. "We must talk in private."

"What?" Marika looked startled. "I don't—"

"Let's go inside." Renee straightened and began walking away.

Moving with the same effortless grace, the other two vampires turned and headed into the house. No one, not even Renee, watched to see if Beck or Marika followed.

They exchanged a glance. Then, with a shrug, Marika turned and headed after them.

Liking this less and less, he followed. When he'd begun this journey with Marika, he'd had no plans of being the lone representative of his entire species.

As they stepped inside the kitchen, a cell phone sitting on the counter chirped.

Renee started for it, but, moving so fast she was a blur, Marika beat her and snatched it up.

"A text message from Brigid," she said. "It says we have to leave."

Glancing at Renee, Beck surmised a look of pure terror on her perfect features.

"It said leave now." Marika turned and stalked out of the room. "Come on."

Beck debated half a second before following her.

Outside, moving fast, she made it halfway up the hillside by the time he caught her.

He opened his mouth to speak. Before he could, the house below them exploded.

The blast knocked them both to the ground.

Stunned, Beck managed to scramble to his feet. Marika had already gotten up. She appeared unhurt.

They both stared at the fire raging below.

"Did you know about this?" he demanded.

"No." She bit her lip. "Of course not."

"Regardless, they don't deserve to die.

They're still inside," he rasped, his throat hoarse. "There's no way they got out."

"They should be all right." Though she sounded unconcerned, the tremor in her voice belied her calm expression. "Vampires as old as they are can survive most fire, as long as they get out in time."

"Can you?" He rasped. "I sure as hell can't."

"Then whoever did this must have been targeting you." She sounded mocking. With the same serene expression, she continued to eye the conflagration, as though she truly expected the three vampires to stroll out at any moment.

He found the fact that they didn't telling. "They're dead."

"I doubt it."

Marika's poise irritated him. Suddenly he wanted nothing more than to see that perfect composure slip.

"Does that bother you?" he asked, his voice low. "The fact that Brigid killed them?"

"You don't know that she's behind this."

He had to bite back the fury. "Then who else, Marika? Who else knew we were in there?"

"If those three were going against us, then the explosion was a good thing. And believe me, as long as they don't burn to ash, they will survive. We continually rise from the dead, you know that."

"I also know that fire is the only thing that will kill vampires."

She inclined her head. "Fire is a true enemy to both of our kinds. But I don't think anyone—Brigid in particular—was trying to kill you. Why would she?"

Beck grabbed her, spinning her around to face him. "Maybe because I'm Dani's father."

"Why does that matter?"

"Because whoever has her might be worried that we might create another like her. Hasn't that thought occurred to you at all?"

She gasped. "What are you saying?"

"Think about it. If we made a child with her abilities once, who's to say we couldn't do it again?"

Her alabaster complexion never changed. But then, vampires couldn't blush unless they'd recently fed.

Another explosion came from below, a smaller one, something catching inside the burning house. The flames continued to roar. There was no local fire department, not way out here. By the time one got here from the closest town, the house would have burned to the ground.

Staring at the fire, Marika appeared to be trying to will the others out. No one emerged as the fire continued to blaze. The wind carried sparks to nearby trees, lighting them like matches.

Still intent on watching for the others, Marika stood alone. Though she appeared composed, he saw how much her show of strength cost her. He sensed she barely held on to the ragged edges of her composure.

"We'd better go," he told her.

"We've got to wait for the others."

"No one, vampire or otherwise, could have survived an explosion and fire that intense. Face it, your friends are not coming out."

"Stop calling them my friends." One corner of her mouth twisted, though her gaze never wavered from the flames. "I told you, Renenet is over a thousand years old. Fire can't touch her. The other two are over five hundred, which means they should be safe, too."

"Then where are they?"

"I don't know. I don't know what's taking them so long."

In the distance, sirens sounded. Finally. The nearest fire department to the rescue. Someone must have seen the explosion and called them.

"We've got to go," he urged again. "Before the humans show up."

"I know, I know." Agitated, she stalked back and forth, still watching the house burn. "Just give me one more minute."

He wanted to wrap her in his arms and quiet her, to press his mouth against the perfect, slender column of her throat and whisper assurances. Instead, he honored her request and held his silence.

One more minute became two, then three. From this height, they could see the road. Lights flashing, a fire truck turned onto it.

"Come on." Grabbing her arm, he headed down, toward the house. More specifically, toward the pickup.

"We have to get out now."

Though she climbed into the truck with him, Marika never stopped watching the house.

Starting the engine, he shifted into Drive and pulled quickly away. "If you're certain they can survive this fire, why are you so determined to see them leave?"

"Because I want to know. I don't want to be responsible for their deaths." Turning in the seat, she continued to watch over her shoulder until the house disappeared from view.

"You're not. Brigid is."

"Again, you don't know that."

"Do you have a better explanation?" he asked.

"Natural causes?" she shot back. "Maybe there was a gas leak or something. Such accidents do happen."

"True." He let his disbelief show in his voice. "And in a similar vein, you never know about the three vamps. Maybe they've already taken off."

"We would have seen them." She sounded exhausted.

"Not if they went out the front while we were still stunned from the explosion. You know how fast you vamps can move."

Silent, she leaned back against the seat and closed her eyes. "That's possible, I guess," she finally conceded. "But why wouldn't they regroup with us?"

"Maybe they got new instructions from Brigid."

"Hmmph. I'm getting tired of Brigid pulling our strings like we're all her marionettes."

He wanted to see her smile. "Maybe they turned into bats and flew away."

Instead of laughing, she shook her head. "That's a myth. We can't do that. I wish we could, though. Sometimes it would sure make things easier."

As they rounded the first curve in the road, the fire truck passed them, lights flashing and siren wailing. Behind it came a smaller truck that served as an ambulance.

"What now?" Beck asked, once the siren had faded into the distance. "What did Brigid tell you to do?"

"She didn't." Her flat voice spoke of her despair. "She gave me no instructions whatsoever, other than meeting with them. In fact, the only new order I heard was for you, when Renee told you to contact your Pack leaders."

He raised a brow. "What else are you not telling me? You're hiding something more. I can sense it."

"What, can you read minds now?"

Waiting patiently, he didn't bother to reply.

"Fine. I'm a witch, too," she snapped.

"A witch?" He shot her a look of disgust. "One more thing you neglected to tell me. If you're a witch, then why haven't you used your powers to help find Dani?"

"Because I have no powers." She swallowed hard, then met his gaze, hers direct. "And that was my last secret. When I was a girl, Brigid was going to train me, until she determined my power wasn't strong enough."

"Still, a witch." He gave her a half smile. "That's something."

"Not really. Obviously, I'm not much of one since I can't even hear my own daughter calling me." She shook her head, her expression bitter. "I'd give anything if I could use magic to locate Dani."

Chapter 7

After her defiantly self-pitying pronounce-
ment, Beck's only reaction was a grunt. Typi-
cal male, though for some reason, this made a
knot form in the pit of Marika's stomach, which
thoroughly pissed her off.

What did she care what Beck thought anyway? But, she realized, she did. He was, despite
everything else, her daughter's father. That
would never change.

The tires hummed on the pavement as they
drove, eating up the miles as the truck air conditioner blew lackluster air, barely cool.

Beck stared straight ahead, concentrating

on the road, still silent. She wanted some kind of reaction. After all, she'd just told him one of her biggest secrets, and he'd barely raised a brow. Worse, he, who had no magic, had been able to hear Dani while she hadn't.

"That's it? All you have to say?"

One corner of his mouth twisted in what could have been a grin or a grimace. "So you're a witch. I've known a few others, though they were human. Nice people. No big deal. But you know what? Maybe you being a vampire witch has something to do with Dani's powers."

"What do you mean?"

"Put a vampire witch together with a shifter and bam. You get pregnant and the child we make together is something the likes of which the world has never seen."

The thought had occurred to her several times, but she'd always dismissed it. "Maybe, but honestly, I'm not that powerful. What little magic I have is barely a spark, not even a flame. Obviously."

He gave her a long look. "Stop beating yourself up over not being able to hear Dani. There could have been a thousand reasons for that."

"Let's hear them."

"Interference."

"What do you mean?"

"Someone could have been trying to keep you from hearing."

"Someone?" Intrigued despite herself, she cocked her head. "Like who?"

"Brigid comes to mind. If she's as powerful as you say, she'd have no problem accomplishing such a thing."

"But for what reason? She wants us to find Dani, if only so she can control her."

"I'm not sure of that. And I think you have more magic than you realize. You can't completely discount the possibility. Vampires just don't get pregnant. It's extremely likely magic played a huge part in this."

"Maybe." She gave him a half smile. "Vampires also don't often mate with shifters."

With a heavy sigh, she turned in her seat and glanced at the dashboard clock. Though the cracked plastic face was dirty, she could still make out the time. "When are you going to call your Pack leaders?"

The seat creaked as Beck shifted his weight. "I don't know. Soon, but I want to wait until I hear back from Simon."

"Your friend? I think you need to go higher. When a full vampire council meets, you know something serious is going on."

"Simon's a Protector. That's pretty high up there." He rolled his eyes. "Higher than that is way out of my comfort zone."

The cell phone rang, as if on cue, making her jump.

Exchanging a quick look with Marika, Beck answered. After a moment, he covered the mouthpiece with his hand. "Senator Jacob Allen's secretary asked me to hold for him. How's that for high?"

"What do you mean? Is this senator part of your Pack?"

"Yes. A highly placed one." He shrugged. "Someone—I'm guessing Brigid—has already gotten the wheels turning and started contacting the upper echelon in the Pack. Hello, yes. Senator?"

Curious, Marika listened. She couldn't tell much from his side of the conversation, since he said little. She supposed she ought to feel honored that beings of authority were getting involved in her daughter's capture, but she couldn't. Years of experience with bureaucracy had taught her that.

When Beck finally completed his call, she crossed her arms. "Well? What did he want? Does he know anything about who took Dani or where we might find her?"

"No." Beck swallowed. "He doesn't."

"Then what did he say?" She touched his hand, her long fingernails scarlet against the luster of his amber skin. "What did he want?"

"To tell me that there'd been another abduction. Another child was taken. Another Halfling." He swallowed hard, his jaw clenching.

For a moment, everything froze. Hugging her arms to her, forcing herself to concentrate, she eyed the movement of his throat, the rise and fall of his muscular chest as he breathed, almost afraid to hear what he'd say next, though she suspected she already knew.

She *knew*. Though she couldn't say how, she simply knew. "When you say the child is another Halfling, you mean one like my Dani, half vampire and half shifter, isn't she?"

"He," he corrected. "And yes, you're right. He's exactly like Dani. Even to what he becomes when he changes. Another griffon. The only difference is that his mother's the shifter and the father is the vampire. And he's a year older than her."

Another griffon.

Feeling as though she'd been dropped into a surreal landscape, she tried to regain her bearings. She was still sitting in the passenger seat of the truck, moving down the deserted highway. Outside, the impossibly clear landscape streaked past, road and dust and dry, yellow grass. To the left, the jagged crags and mysterious mountains. High above, bright sunlight lit the blue, blue sky. Next to her sat an impossibly handsome man, his chiseled features clouded with concern. She had the oddest sense of completion, something she didn't want or need right now.

"Are you all right?" he asked, his voice calm, his gaze steady.

Her rock. She pushed the thought away.

"Yes. No." Hand to her throat, she shifted in her seat. "How is this possible?"

"I don't know, but I'm beginning to see why so many higher-ups are getting involved. The senator seemed really concerned about Dani and what she can do. He even called her a griffon."

"So did I." Suddenly weary, she closed her eyes. "If there are two, there might be more."

"And no one knows why these people are kidnapping them." He touched her shoulder, making her jump.

"That's what I don't understand, either." The question had haunted her ever since they'd gotten to Addie's, and she'd realized her daughter was missing. "Why are they doing this?"

"The senator said something about other powers. You mentioned when Dani changed, she could fly. Did she have any other powers? Any of your magic?"

"No." Marika closed her eyes, picturing her raven-haired, chubby, laughing child. "She's just a sweet little girl, my baby." Her voice cracked. "We've got to find her."

"The senator said that, with her abilities, they think Dani and the boy might be dangerous." His voice was gentle, as though afraid she might break.

But this outraged her. She gave him a look of disbelief. "Dangerous? She's not even three. I can't believe…" Then, collecting herself, she lifted her chin and continued. "Did he know who grabbed them, or why?"

"If he did, he didn't tell me. He mentioned something about giving us a briefing once the National Pack Council finished meeting."

"The National Pack Council is meeting?" Even she knew how big this was. As big as the Vampire Council meeting. If both species were this worried, they had to know something she didn't. She couldn't shake the feeling she had missed something, some clue, some hint, *something*. But what?

"Yep. I don't know who contacted them, but this is huge."

"Hugely weird. Things moved fast for that level of bureaucracy," she mused. "Maybe now that they're involved, they can help us figure out where the children are."

"Anything's possible. But the only problem with that is if they figure out where, they'll send special forces. Like Protectors."

"And Huntresses," she agreed. Then, studying him, she sighed. Something in his face… "That's not a problem. Or is it? What else are you not telling me?"

"Well," he said slowly, "whoever snatched that kid took the parents, too."

This was a shock. But then again, they'd captured both her and Beck, too. "What? The parents?"

"That would explain why they grabbed both of us."

"But I thought they wanted us to tell them how to find Dani."

"They did. But they wanted us, too."

"I don't understand. Why?"

"Not sure." His expression made it plain he didn't like what he had to tell her next. "The senator seemed to think...maybe for breeding purposes."

Breeding purposes. As if she could ever replicate Dani. Not in a thousand years. She shook her head.

"But this was a fluke, wasn't it? A onetime thing. If you and I had stayed together and if, miraculously, we'd had more children, would they all have been little...griffons?"

This time when Beck looked at her, something intense blazed in his amber eyes. "I don't know. It's possible. The senator said something about your safety."

"My safety?" She brushed off that concern. "I'm a Huntress. I can take care of myself."

"You've been captured once."

"You had to point that out, didn't you?" She smiled wryly. "I *was* in danger. So were you. But we escaped. I don't think they'll bother us again."

"They won't, but there are others. We don't know how many are involved."

Again he'd managed to shock her. "You think more than one group wanted Dani?"

"I don't know. There are shifters involved here and vampires. Normally, the two groups don't work together."

"Again, why? Why my little girl?"

"This griffon ability apparently changes things."

"How?"

"You're a witch, you tell me. Use your magic."

Her inelegant snort showed him what she thought of that. "I already told you, my magic is limited and extremely unreliable."

"Listen to me. They grabbed the other parents. It's reasonable to think they want you, too, to make more little griffons." Again he touched her arm. She bit the side of her cheek to keep from curling into his hand.

She managed a laugh, short and completely without humor. "Why just me? You're part of this equation, too. And then, assuming they succeed and breed more little…griffons. Then what? They'd do what with them? Seriously, so Dani becomes a flying wolf? So what? She's different, not an ordinary shifter, but still. She has no superpowers."

Raising a brow, he also lifted one shoulder. "I don't know. She's young. You have no idea what else she might be able to do when she gets older."

"True, but neither do they. She's two and the boy is three. Why grab them now? Why not wait until they're older?"

"So they can train them. It's like in the Protectors. They take us when we're four years old. We're raised up living with them, being fed a steady diet of doctrine."

"You sound bitter."

He shrugged. "Maybe a little."

"Some of what you said makes sense. But there are only two children. Not enough to make an army, surely."

"Unless there were others." He cleared his throat. "Other children, older than Dani, who'd already been captured years ago and are growing up there."

"Oh, no." His words brought an almost physical pain. But the idea, so shocking at first, made a sort of twisted sense the more she considered it. "Their poor parents. But if that's the case, why haven't the children been reported missing? Surely we would have heard."

"Unless," he said slowly, "the parents were captured, too."

"And what, killed?"

"Maybe." From the grim set of his mouth, she guessed he definitely believed this possibility.

"Why would they do that? Why would anyone do that?"

He sighed. "We don't know how they think. They might have killed the parents to keep them quiet about the kids. Or they could be using the parents for breeding purposes, as I mentioned earlier. One male could service numerous women."

She was old enough that most things didn't

shock her. But this was personal and appalling. "Like a puppy mill, only with children?"

"Exactly." He frowned. "Though I'd be surprised if someone hasn't tried that already. There'd be more griffons. We'd have heard something."

"Good luck to them with that idea." She made her voice flat. "Of course it won't work. There's more involved than just breeding. Also, if they tried to use me that way, or any vampire for that matter, they'd die trying."

The quick flash of his smile told her he could relate. "Still, they drugged you once. They could do so again. You need to be careful."

"Me, careful?" She laughed. "Actually, I'd rather they *do* capture me. At least that way I could be with my baby girl."

He didn't reply, instead tightening his hands on the wheel until his knuckles showed white.

A fleeting urge, a bit of temporary insanity came over her. She wanted to lean over and touch him, to smooth the frown lines from his forehead, to use her fingertips to ease the tightness of his mouth. Crazy.

She sighed. "This senator, what did he want us to do?"

"He wanted us to wait. He said we'd receive instructions later, when we were briefed. Right now, the most powerful of both of our kinds are meeting. Your Brigid is involved again—that woman has her fingers in every piece of pie. He wants us to give them a chance to work something out."

"Wait?" She couldn't believe him. "Is he insane?"

He shot her a look. "I don't know, but I've never been much for waiting, myself. How about you?"

"We have no information, not even a hint. What can we do?" Despite her skepticism, she couldn't keep the hope from her voice.

"We'll get information. Go to the source."

"Now you're talking." Finally. She sat up straight, invigorated at the thought of finally doing something. "What did you have in mind?"

His savage grin made him look devilishly handsome. "I'm tired of doing nothing. They won't come to us, so we'll go to them."

"Got to who?"

"Where does Brigid hang out?"

"I don't know. I've only met her at school.

I've never been to her home. If Renee and the others were still here, they might know."

Pulling over to the side of the road, he turned in his seat to face her. As usual, his rugged, masculine beauty took her breath away. And, as usual, she had to struggle to pretend to be unaffected.

"How about we try to find her? You said these mountains are a virtual vampire enclave, right?"

She blinked, then gave him a slow smile. "Yes, but there are a lot of miles to cover. I can use my senses to detect the power of the vampire inside, but if we have to talk to anyone, you'll have to let me do the talking. The vampires won't appreciate your presence."

"They'll get used to the idea. Are you sure you're up for that?"

"What else do we have to do?" She managed a resolute smile, wondering how he could still affect her so strongly. "I don't know about you, but if I do nothing but sit around and wait for them to contact us, I'll go crazy. I want Dani."

His return smile did nothing to help her equilibrium.

"This will be a beginning. And, if we seek

her out, we can show Brigid we don't want to be pushed around."

"True." She knew she didn't sound convinced. "But we need to be careful. For as long as I've been a vampire, Brigid has been High Priestess. No one goes against her and survives. No one."

Grim-faced, he nodded. "Then we'll be the first."

She couldn't help but like his attitude. "Give me the phone. Please."

Slowly, he handed it over. "You're calling Brigid?"

"Yes. If she's so all-knowing, then she's already aware we're trying to find her. Maybe she'd be willing to give us directions." She punched in a number and hit send.

After listening for a moment, she closed the cell and handed it back. "No answer. She's choosing not to answer. That pisses me off. I feel like I'm running in place."

Slanting her a sideways look, he laughed. "Like a hamster on a wheel. I know the feeling. I had it a lot when I worked for the Protectors. That's one of the reasons I quit."

She didn't have a retort for that and fell silent.

Beck drove with the same intense concentration he brought to everything. They traveled up one winding gravel road and down another, stopping for gas once. Onto dead-end streets, mini-ranchettes, more houses perched on cliffs, none yielding what they wanted to find. Though he slowed at each one, letting Marika use her extra senses, she shook her head so many times her neck hurt.

As the sun began to set, he finally pulled the truck over. When he looked at her, his mouth twisted ruefully. "I'm sorry, but I've got to rest. I can sleep while you drive, or we can stop somewhere for the night."

She thought about that for a moment. "The vampires come out more at night. I don't want to be driving around to their houses while they're traveling. We'll stop. Do you mind sleeping outdoors?"

Grinning, he rolled his eyes. "I'm a wolf, remember? Where did you have in mind?"

"Down there." Pointing in the opposite direction, toward the flat desert, she remembered how hard he'd slept full-out, the way he did everything. She'd used to love to hold him while he was asleep and burn his features into her memory. Now, all she could think about was her daughter, about to face the night without her mother or Addie.

He frowned in puzzlement. "Why down there?"

It took her a moment to retrace the conversation.

"We need to get out of the mountains if we're stopping. It's safer down there, out of vampire territory."

"Don't you think we should check with Brigid, see if she has further instructions?"

"No." Her flat reply came quickly. "She said she'd contact me if she learned anything new."

"Okay then." He turned the truck around, following her directions down from the mountains. Once they'd reached level ground, they left the main road, taking a gravel one that appeared to go on forever and lead to nowhere, the desert way ahead.

After a few minutes of bouncing along, she pointed to another dirt track, nearly hidden by towering grass. "There. In about a hundred feet, there's a perfect copse of trees."

He pulled off, parking under a crooked tree. When he turned to look at her, his face was in shadow. "I can catch a few *z*'s in the pickup bed. What about you?"

She tried not to think about how badly she wanted to curl up next to him. "I'll stand guard. I don't need to sleep," she told him, effectively quashing that fantasy. Her longing for her daughter intensified. She wanted Dani so badly it hurt to breathe.

She swallowed, almost afraid to ask. "Will you try again to hear her?"

He blinked. "There's no wind."

"Still, please listen." Though she hated sounding as if she was begging, for Dani she'd do anything. "Just try."

Rolling his shoulders back, he took a deep breath and lifted his face to the sky. Cocking his head, he closed his eyes.

While she clutched her hands together and waited.

Finally, he opened his eyes. "Nothing. I'm sorry."

The ring of despair in his voice echoed the one inside of her. She tried to summon a smile and failed. "Hey, at least you tried. Now you'd better get some rest."

Yawning, he nodded, found an old blanket to wrap around himself and crawled into the back of the pickup to sleep.

To save her soul, Marika couldn't help but envy him. Sleeping brought forgetfulness, a peace she hadn't had in centuries. Maybe if she listened hard enough, she'd hear her daughter in the stillness of the night.

Hoping that would be the case, she climbed up on the hood of the pickup and perched there to stand guard.

Beck slept deeply, waking to a still-black sky with stars sparkling like a thousand tiny flashlights. Though he usually had vivid dreams, what dreams he could remember had been erotic, fragmented flashes of silky skin and willing mouths. But as he struggled back to consciousness, fully aroused and aching for Marika, he knew he'd have to will his body back to normal before facing her.

Grateful both for the night and for the fact that he'd kept his jeans on, he rolled onto his side to discover her lying next to him, fully clothed and wide awake.

"Hey," he rasped, wishing he had a blanket to cover his lower body.

Her devilish smile told him she'd already noticed. "Good morning. The sun will rise soon."

Looking where she pointed, he saw that the eastern horizon glowed a dusky rose, the exact color of her lips. Hellhounds. He struggled to find something to say, anything that would take his mind off the flashes of erotic images he could still see in his head.

He gave her a sideways glance. She appeared comfortable and serene, bathed in rosy dawn light and looking so lovely he wanted to kiss her. And more.

Damn it.

Biting back a groan, he knew he needed to distract himself. "We need to get going."

"True." With a fluid motion, she rose. "I'm ready if you are."

Just like that. He envied her that she didn't need sleep, appreciating that she hadn't begrudged them stopping so he could rest.

Stretching, he smothered a yawn. "I'd kill for some coffee."

"We'll get some at the first place we come to."

With that promise, he rubbed the sleep out of his eyes and climbed out of the pickup bed, sliding into the driver's seat and struggling to focus on the road.

Starting the truck, he moved restlessly, then shifted into Drive and pulled out onto the road. "Talk to me. Help me wake up."

He'd barely finished his sentence when his cell phone rang. Checking the caller ID, he grimaced. "Brigid," he told Marika before answering.

"I dreamed of a grave," Brigid said. "Someone close to you both. Who?"

"My sister." Throat closed, he swallowed back a curse.

"I see. And did she know about the child?"

"No." Then, despite his denial, he couldn't help but glance at Marika.

"Then what is the connection?"

"You're the seer," he retorted. "You tell me."

"Talk to the Huntress. Perhaps if the two of

you can search your memories, you might find the answer, the tie." And she ended the call.

"Well?" Eyes narrowed, Marika studied him. "What did she say?"

"That we should talk about Juliet. Something about there being a connection. She didn't know about Dani, of course."

"No." Marika frowned. "I don't see how Jules had anything to do with this."

"Me, either." Glancing at her, he shrugged. "But we've never talked about it. Maybe we should."

"If Brigid thinks this will help…"

"Then we will."

He took a deep breath. Talking about such a painful subject definitely helped him wake up. "Juliet and I grew up with only each other to rely on. As you know, we were both trained as Protectors, taken away from our parents at the tender age of four. This made us closer than most other siblings. We had no secrets from each other. None whatsoever. Or I believed."

"What happened?" she asked softly, though she was sure she already knew.

Lost in memories, he didn't respond immediately. For the first time in months, his inner wolf had been growing restless. Now, awakened by the sharp stab of Beck's desire, the wolf wanted out. "We were so close. So when Juliet announced she was leaving the Society, I was stunned and, then later, furious. Not so much at her choice, but at the realization that she'd obviously been struggling with this decision for months. In secret."

"That must have been difficult."

Though he heard no mockery in her silky smooth voice, he found himself searching her expression anyway. Eyes still closed, she sat motionless, like a sleeping beauty waiting for a kiss to wake her. His kiss.

Renewed heat shot through him at the idea. Again, he knew he had to continue talking or he'd be in deep trouble. And if there really was a clue here somewhere, he didn't want to miss it.

"That wasn't even the worst of it. When I asked, Jules went on the defensive. She attacked me, every vulnerable insecurity I had. And she knew them all."

Remembering this, what he'd tried so hard to forget, still hurt like a festering sore deep inside, even after all these years. He hadn't understood what had driven Jules then. One of his biggest regrets, other than failing to prevent her death, had been not knowing about or being able to help her with her crisis of faith.

Taking a deep breath, he gripped the steering wheel and forced himself to go on. "Then when Juliet finished with me, she began denigrating the Protectors, the very organization we'd both dedicated our lives to serving."

He glanced at Marika. Her eyes were open. Staring at him, she sat up straight, her expression soft and puzzled. "That doesn't sound like the Jules I knew."

"She wasn't herself that day. I was hurt. Furious, too." He gave her a sideways glance, glad there was no traffic on the road.

Marika nodded, but he sensed she didn't understand. How could she? Not only had he chosen his job over searching for her and making things right between them, she'd never had to come to terms with the knowledge that every ideal he'd held dear, every belief he'd felt certain about, had been based on lies.

The Protectors had let him down, just as he'd let her down.

Still, he felt he had to admit all this to her,

maybe as a form of penance. "When she stormed out of there that day, I thought my baby sister hated me. Later, I learned she'd been ordered and forced to exterminate a Feral against her better judgment. Now, I can actually relate, but then I was still besotted with the Protectors' organization."

She touched his hand again, and for a moment, he barely remembered to breathe. If circumstances had been different, he would have kissed her then.

"Juliet never told me about that," she said, her voice soft and hurt. "And I still don't see how this has anything to do with my daughter."

"Our daughter," he corrected. "Humor me. We have to keep talking. Maybe then we can figure this out."

"Then continue. Juliet was hurt?"

"Yes. She was like a wounded wolf, snarling in pain. She apologized later. We made up, went on. She quit the Protectors. I didn't understand then. I do now."

"You quit, too, right?"

"Sort of." Saying the words brought a sad heaviness to his chest. "I'm on a leave of absence. I haven't decided what I'm going to d—"

She started to speak, then cocked her head, listening.

In the distance, a noise. He knew that sound.

"Hear that?" He cracked his window, listening. After a moment, she nodded.

The faint reverberation in the distance sounded like a helicopter. Years of using them in his missions had made it easy to identify them.

A moment later, his suspicions were confirmed. A military chopper appeared on the horizon, heading straight for them.

Friend? Or foe? Protectors or something else?

He hadn't contacted anyone, therefore he had no choice but to assume the worst.

Chapter 8

Acting on pure instinct, he hit the brake and twisted the wheel, sending them off-road. "No way we can outrun them. We've got to hide."

The chopper neared. They were out in the open, their pickup completely exposed, a black spot against the brown desert floor. Accelerating, he pointed them toward the nearest group of twisted mesquite trees, a good fifty to sixty yards away.

The chopper grew closer, the sound shaking the ground.

As soon as they reached the protective shadow of the trees, Beck slowed. He let the pickup coast into the shade, putting it in Park, though he didn't kill the engine. He cursed. "I'm sure they spotted us."

"How do you know they're not your guys?" she asked, level-voiced.

He gave her a sharp look, thought about telling her he didn't have any guys and then shrugged. "I don't. I have no idea who's in that helicopter, whether they're friend or foe."

The chopper landed in the meadow near the spot where they'd gone off-road, sending dust and rock scurrying across the dry grass.

The blades were still whirling as two men emerged. Tall, pale and elegant, they looked as if they'd stepped from the pages of a historical novel, despite modern clothes and expensive, wraparound sunglasses.

Though they were a good fifty yards away, they appeared to be staring straight at them.

"Not Protectors," she said.

"Worse," Beck groaned. "More vampires."

Still intently watching them, she smiled. "I can't tell if they're young or old. Either way, I don't know them. But there's a shifter, too," she pointed. "Look."

Sure enough, another man appeared in the

doorway. He dropped to the ground and began moving toward them with a confident, long-legged stride that was instantly familiar.

Simon. Beck felt a rush of surprise, followed by relief.

"That's a friend of mine." Now he killed the ignition, pushing open his door and stepping outside. A second later, he heard Marika do the same, though she remained under the shelter of the trees.

The two men met halfway, with the vampires hanging back.

They embraced, clapping each other on the back. When they broke apart, Beck grinned at his friend. "I should've known you'd show up."

"Why? Did you think I was already bored with married life?" Simon's rakish grin put that idea to rest. A few months ago, he'd met and married his mate, a formerly Feral shifter named Raven.

Marika glided up to them, her beautiful face expressionless. She trained most of her attention on the two vampires.

"You must be Marika?" Simon smiled at her, moving forward when she held out her hand.

Instead of taking it, he hugged her, too. "Any close friend of Beck is a close friend of mine."

Though her perfectly arched brows rose, she gave no other indication of surprise. She coolly endured Simon's hug, stepping back quickly once it was over, her gaze returning to the two vampires.

When they made no move toward her, she went to them, her posture rigid and tense despite her fluid movements.

"I am the Huntress Marika," she said, her voice formal. Dipping the upper half of her body in a semibow, she waited for them to acknowledge her and give their names.

Instead, they silently stared at her, expressions carved from stone, eyes unreadable behind the dark glasses.

Beck glanced at Simon, who shrugged. "They wouldn't even talk to me," he said. "Maybe they don't speak the language."

"How'd you all end up on the same chopper?"

"Assignment. I reported as instructed, they showed up and we took off."

"The Protectors *assigned* you to me?" Stunned, Beck forgot about the others. "Why?"

"You called me."

"As a friend, not as a Protector."

"I'm both. You know that."

Beck acknowledged the accuracy of those words. "True. Now that you're here, what are you supposed to do?'

Instead of Simon, one of the vampires answered. Somehow they'd moved closer without Beck even noticing.

"We're taking you to Brigid," the vamp said, his smooth voice carrying the lilting intonations of a far-off land.

To Brigid? Exactly as they'd wanted.

Still, something felt wrong.

"Hey." Simon nudged him. "No worries, man. Pack council leaders are there, too. It's some sort of full-fledged crisis, though I haven't been briefed yet. At HQ, there're all sorts of rumors floating around. End of the world and all that."

After a quick glance at Simon, Beck again looked at Marika. "Marika and I need a moment alone," he said.

After throwing up his hands and muttering something that sounded like "pigheaded," Simon nodded and went to stand near the vampires, who stepped closer to Beck, apparently not understanding.

"Come on." Simon grabbed the closest one's arms. "Back off. Give them some space."

The vamp glowered at him. "Take your hands off me."

When Simon did, he glided back over to his buddy.

"Five minutes," he said, glaring at Beck. "No more."

Beck wanted to ask "Or what?" but didn't. No sense in starting trouble if it wasn't necessary.

He and Marika moved into the trees, stopping only when they couldn't be overheard.

"I know we wanted to find Brigid, but I've got a bad feeling about this," Beck said.

"Like you did right before the house exploded?"

He nodded.

She leaned in, so close her long hair brushed against his arm. "You know, while I'm seriously beginning to doubt Brigid's intentions, I don't know. If she can help us…"

"Renenet was trying to tell you something right before Brigid called," he said. "When you told her Brigid was texting, she looked absolutely terrified."

"Brigid has that effect on people." Studying her hands, she considered. "You know what? I trust you. If you don't think we should go, then we won't. All I care about is finding Dani. If Brigid is trying to get in our way, then by all means, we should avoid her."

He felt mildly guilty. What if he was wrong? Their daughter's life was at stake.

He had to stop second-guessing himself. Ever since he'd learned of the corruption in the Protectors, he'd doubted his own judgment.

"I'll play devil's advocate. We might need to talk to Brigid, find out what she knows, though that could prove dangerous. And Simon said Pack council is with her, as well as some of the upper vampire echelon."

Dark eyes shadowed, she considered his words. "I don't have time for political games, unless they could help us find Dani." She fingered a wayward strand of her hair, making his fingers itch to smooth it back. "Maybe we should split up. I'll go, you stay here."

For a second, his heart stopped. "No. We stay together."

She studied him. "You're probably right. Okay. Do you trust him?" she whispered, indicating Simon.

"Implicitly." Beck didn't even hesitate. "Who are the two vamps?"

"Two of Brigid's personal guard. They're very powerful."

"In what way? Magic?"

"Yes. Though most vampires aren't magical, some are. Brigid only surrounds herself with those who have magic. And before you ask, I don't know them well enough to trust them. Since Dani was born, I've lived my life making it a practice not to trust anyone I didn't know."

She glanced again at Simon. "Did your friend tell you what they want with us?"

"No." Beck eyed Simon's unsmiling face first, then those of the two vampires. "I asked, but he said he hadn't been briefed yet. He was sent by the Protectors.

"He still works for them?"

"Yes. They've cleaned up their act."

She watched him closely. "Do you trust them?"

"If I don't, it has more to do with my nature than with them. Because of what happened in the past, I have trouble believing anything they say."

Uncertainty colored her voice. "And we have no real proof that Brigid isn't on our side. I think we should go. We wanted to talk to Brigid anyway."

"Just don't let your guard down."

Acknowledging his warning with a nod, she motioned to the vamps, who glided closer, side by side. "We're ready."

The dark-headed one nodded, then whispered, "Renenet says to say hello."

Marika drew back. "I knew we should have checked the site for survivors. She lives?"

"Yes. She, Heh and Usi survived the fire. A bit scorched, but none the worse for wear." He glanced at Beck. "She has asked me to tell you to be careful."

Beck couldn't hide his surprise. "We want to talk to her. Will she be at this meeting?"

The vampire looked away. "No. You will see her later."

As they climbed on the helicopter, Beck took a seat beside Simon, pulling Marika next to him. Except for her, he couldn't help but notice they sat in two groups and wondered if Simon also felt outnumbered. If it came to a battle, shifters versus vampires, he and Simon would be sure to lose.

As the helicopter flight north jarred Marika's teeth, she wondered how the pilot planned to land it in the mountains. Assuming Brigid's stronghold was there. She was pretty sure it was. She also couldn't help but wonder why the great witch vampire had found it necessary to capture them rather than simply issuing a summons. It seemed she could have crooked one magical finger, and they would have done as she asked. They had so far.

Unless Brigid had somehow gotten wind of their mistrust. Again, she wondered about the explosion and whether Brigid had truly caused it.

Only Renenet knew for sure. Her absence from the meeting seemed telling.

Eyeing the two vamps sitting motionless, despite the jarring ride, she couldn't help but watch Beck. Compared to the vampires—and she had to include herself in that category— he seemed so vital, so alive. She wondered what he saw when he looked at her. A cold, hollowed-out shell of a female, or was he able to see past her pale exterior to the woman blazing inside?

Sometimes, she caught him looking and thought he did see inside her. This was more tempting to her than the finest blood but also infinitely more dangerous.

She couldn't afford to let anything or anyone distract her from finding Dani.

Still, her traitorous heart couldn't help but wonder what would happen once they found Dani. Granted, Beck would be a part of their daughter's life, but would he still want to be a part of hers?

The helicopter dipped, sending her stomach in the opposite direction. While she regained her equilibrium, Beck turned in his seat, his expression concerned.

"Are you all right?"

Conscious of the vampires beside her, she nodded. "Fine," she said coolly. "How about you?"

"I'm good." He touched her hand. "We're nearly there, I think."

Again the chopper dropped as they headed

toward a flat-topped mesa. Beck was right. They must be close to landing.

When they cleared a stand of trees, and she saw a meadow below with a perfect circle of cement, she had a flash of memory. She'd been here before.

As she peered out the side, Marika took in flashes of color. Bright sunlight sparkling on the impossibly vivid green grass, in direct contrast to the dry brown dust of desert mountains.

Like a bird settling in its nest, the chopper eased down and landed. Then, she saw the temple. Made of native earth and cedar, the structure rose to the sky as though giving praise. She *had* been here before, though until this very moment, she'd thought her memories of the breathtakingly beautiful structure were cloudy remnants from a dream.

Had Brigid's magic been responsible for that?

Beside her, Beck drew in his breath, and she knew he'd seen Brigid's place, too. He took her arm, and they exited, letting the vampires go first, Simon following, and she and Beck bringing up the rear.

A few more steps and she nearly staggered.

She sensed power long before they reached the entrance to the house. Rolling off the place in blatant waves, so strong it made walking difficult.

As if he understood, Beck took her arm. He seemed to have no difficulties. Arm in arm, they climbed the steps and approached the carved oak double doors, their escorts pausing and letting them go past, then staying close on their heels.

A low swell of noise rose from behind the doors. Beck tightened his grip and looked at her, a silent question in his gaze. She shrugged and pushed the doors open. Together, they entered the room.

A sea of faces turned toward them. Both stopped. A flutter of panic vibrated in Marika's chest. The chamber was as crowded as a stadium or concert hall, packed to the ceiling. A sold-out event.

Here to see Brigid? Or for the big meeting the other vamps had mentioned?

"Hellhounds," Beck muttered beside her. "The place is full of vampires and shifters, together."

He was right. Not that the two species exactly comingled. One side of the stadium was filled entirely of row after row of vampires, and the other side held only shifters.

She caught herself scanning the crowd for Dani, conscious that beside her, Beck did the same.

And still, power coiled around her, both seductive and dangerous, making thought difficult.

"If anyone wanted to exterminate the most powerful of our kind, now would be the time to do it," Beck muttered in her ear.

"I'm sure they have magic in place to prevent that," she whispered back. He raised a brow, as if surprised.

"Apparently you can't feel the swell of power that's surrounding us?"

He shook his head. "I take it you can?"

"Yes," she said simply. "It's insinuating itself into my every pore.

"Follow us." One of their vampire escorts led them to what would have been the infield in a stadium. Beck glanced over his shoulder, and she did, too. Beck's friend, Simon, kept pace with them, an impassive soldier.

Still, everyone else in the building maintained their awful, heavy silence. Each footstep sounded like a jackhammer, and the stare of so many eyes stung like laser pricks of light.

As they crossed between the floor seats and headed up to a stage, Marika noted one difference in the way those occupying this particular area had chosen their seats.

No longer segregated, they were next to each other. Mixed, two of one species here, one of another, then three more. Here, vampires comingling with shifters, one-to-one, not separated into groups of any kind, and plainly equals.

Here were the really powerful ones.

Beck squeezed her arm, silently noting the difference, as well. His tension, nearly as palpable as the magic, warned her not to let down her guard.

As if she would. Being here felt ten times more dangerous than she'd anticipated.

As they approached the stage area, the crowds murmuring and talking swelled again, before abruptly dying down as Beck took her hand.

Again, in complete silence, the gathering of vamps and shifters watched Marika and

Beck and their escorts climb the steps to the raised dais.

The platform was empty. A long table, carved of polished marble, ran the length of the stage, easily fifty feet. Chairs lined one side only, and in a sole nod to modern technology, microphones had been strategically placed at intervals of five feet.

Again, Marika sensed a protective shield surrounding the table.

Their escorts left them then, disappearing as completely as if they'd melted away. Simon moved to stand slightly behind Beck, sending her a dark look that managed to convey a promise of help if they needed it.

Marika felt absurdly grateful.

For a moment, she and Beck stood alone, surrounded by the sea of strangers. If a spotlight had highlighted them in a blaze of brilliant yellow, she wouldn't have been surprised. This circus felt both surreal and too realistic at once.

As they waited, others entered from the back of the stage, like performers. They wore matching robes in a brown as rich as melted chocolate. Here, too, species mingled, entering alternately so that it was shifter, vamp, shifter, vamp.

"Councils," Beck said, low-voiced. "Joint councils meeting together. The rarest of rare events."

As each took their place at the table, she felt the steady increase of power building. This could only mean one thing. The High Priestess Vampire was approaching.

This meant Brigid would enter last, her position clearly revealing her as the most powerful.

In case anyone doubted. Meeting her, most did not.

Beside Marika, Beck stood at wary attention. For a brief instant, she tore her attention away from the procession slowly filing past them and looked at him. As she did, the room temperature dropped, and his expression altered, freezing into a grimace as though ice seeped into every pore.

Brigid had entered.

Marika swung her head around to eye the center of the dais. The old one's gaze seared her. Brigid had been studying her, sizing her up.

Rolling back her shoulders, Marika lifted

her chin. The least she could do was return the favor.

Brigid's flawless beauty had hardened with unimaginable age. Her porcelain skin appeared dusted by frost. Her emerald eyes and her painted lips were the only slashes of color in the perfect oval of her face.

They stared at each other so long that others began to notice. Even Beck turned to look at Marika. She ignored him, unwilling or unable to be the first to concede.

Gaze still locked with Marika's, Brigid finally took her seat. Though ancient, her fluid movements only added to her aching beauty, a legacy from her Fae ancestry. Through the aeons, no doubt many men, both human and vampire, had fallen under her spell.

Even Beck appeared transfixed, though he remained at Marika's side.

Finally seated, Brigid looked to her left and then to her right, acknowledging the others and breaking the silent standoff.

Relieved, Marika finally looked down. Her own miniscule power, newly awakened, simmered within her, making her feel…more. Of everything. For the first time in her life, she had to rein herself in, curtail the swell of energy pulsing from her. The stakes were too damn high.

She sensed that Beck, beside her, was having similar difficulties controlling his wolf.

"Welcome." Brigid spoke, her magic rolling off her in waves, crashing up against Marika with such force she nearly staggered back. "We come together to discuss the threat against both our species and the world as we know it."

Marika exchanged a look with Beck. "I'm not sure where she's going with this, but it's exactly what I expected. Vague and alarmist," she murmured.

In response, Beck dipped his chin, watching Brigid and waiting for her to continue.

"Throughout the centuries, in both our species, radical groups have risen and fallen. Many still exist to this day. For the most part, we have been tolerant unless they posed a threat to our survival. Except for the age of wars, we've been able to enact a truce and learn to work together to take care of any threats.

"Until now," she continued. "Now an entirely new species has been birthed."

Marika stiffened. Dani was just Dani. Not

some freak of nature or new species, but her daughter, her baby girl.

Brigid went on to detail what Dani was and what she could do. She also mentioned the boy and then, just when Marika's impatience was about to explode, began to talk about others. Plural. As in, there were more than two.

Brigid cited eleven other documented cases. That meant there were thirteen total. Thirteen children, each of them grabbed by this radical group of shifters.

The crowd erupted. In normal times, accusations might have been hurled at each other, shifter versus vampire, and vice versa. But today, they all seemed to agree with the urgency Brigid conveyed. The stakes were high.

Thirteen missing children were hard to ignore.

"How has this gone unnoticed?" Marika directed her attention to the High Priestess. "If this has been going on for years, surely you must have known about it. Why weren't the parents warned? If I'd known, I could have taken additional steps to protect my daughter. I might have been able to prevent her capture."

Instantly, the crowd quieted, all eyes on Brigid, waiting for her answer.

"I tried to contact you." Brigid gentled the severity of her voice. "But you ignored my summons, choosing to go on the run instead."

"What about the explosion?"

"What about it?" Brigid's smile contained a hint of malice. "We are not here to discuss such trivial matters.

"Your daughter is among those missing. We must get these children gathered up and brought to us. I have seen indications that they, with their special and peculiar abilities, possess great power. Whoever controls them will control their magic."

As Marika was about to speak, Brigid directed her sharp gaze toward her. "The parents cannot be relied on to keep them safe. You are proof of that. Therefore, once we have the children, they'll live here at the temple and begin training immediately."

A swell of agreement came from the assembly, bringing a slight smile of satisfaction to Brigid's aristocratic face.

Only Beck's grip kept Marika from taking a step toward the High Priestess in protest.

She glanced at him. "Not gonna happen," Marika said, though the crowd's noise drowned out her words. "*I* decide how my daughter's raised. She can't—"

"Play along." His tone urgent, Beck leaned in close. "If you disagree, we'll likely become her prisoners."

If Brigid was capable of talking about children as though they were instruments of war, weapons, what was next?

"How will we find them?" someone asked.

Now Brigid flashed a satisfied smile in Marika's direction, looking both beautiful and terrible. "These children have some sort of telepathic ability. Apparently, they continuously try to make contact with the parents. Thus, we've begun taking the parents into custody." She indicated Beck and Marika.

"We'll put them into a force-induced coma. This trancelike state will enable us to initiate contact."

As Marika tried to react—to fight—Brigid's power redoubled, restraining her.

Chapter 9

Beck couldn't move. No matter how hard he strained against the invisible bonds that held him, he couldn't so much as lift a finger.

Inside, his wolf snarled and raged, as infuriated as the human half, desperate to get out.

Still Beck remained human, frozen.

Beside him, Marika came to life.

"Hell, no, you're not," she snarled. "Come on, Beck." She grabbed his arm.

Miraculously, her touch released him. His wolf chose this moment to make a frantic bid for freedom. Somehow, Beck managed to fight his beast back.

"They don't have Dani," she said. "And they don't have any idea how to find her. Come on. We've got to get out of here."

From her thronelike chair, Brigid laughed, a cynical, dry sound. Still laughing, she motioned with her hands and sent another burst of power, full blast, at them.

With Marika still gripping his arm, Beck never felt a thing.

"Don't let go of me," he told her as they hurried away. "You're my protection against her magic."

She nodded and took off, gripping his hand firmly.

They cleared the first hurdle—the steps from the arena floor to the first tier of seats. No one made a move to stop them. Instead, every member of the audience sat rigid in their seats, staring straight ahead, completely ignoring them.

Brigid's magic must have affected them, too, making them oblivious to the magnitude of the crimes being committed right in front of them.

Perfect. He had the fleeting thought that maybe Brigid was making escape too easy but let it go for now. First, they had to break out.

Then they could discuss the possibility that she was toying with them.

Hand in hand, they sprinted up the steps and down the long hallway that led to the atrium area. Still held in place by Brigid's spell, no one even questioned them.

They slammed into the outside doors, sending them crashing open. Outside, they never broke stride.

The instant they reached pavement, Beck's wolf broke free.

"No," he cried, not ready. Wolf didn't care. Too much time had passed since the beast had been released. Caged in his human prison far too long, wolf wanted out, needed out, fought claw and nail for his freedom.

Another cry ripping from his throat, Beck dropped to the ground. On all fours, he shuddered, dimly hearing the sound of his clothes tearing.

Then he was wolf. Seeing though his nose more than his eyes, he crouched next to the woman with no scent at all, staring.

Even as wolf, he was conscious of the need to flee. Nudging Marika with his snout, he started off. She grabbed him and, hand clutching his fur, she easily kept up with him. At vampire-wolf speed they ran through a field full of parked cars, across the winding road, and headed up the hill into the trees. Only when they'd cleared the crest and began descending the other side, did he slow to a jog, a walk and then finally, a stop, panting.

Fighting for control, he began the change back to man.

Then, naked, hands on legs, doubled over and trying to catch his breath, he attempted to figure out what had happened. Not since he'd been a young boy had he lost a battle with the beast inside him. The wolf had forced an involuntary change, and Beck didn't like it one bit.

"What happened back there?" Marika demanded. "Why the wolf? You were doing fine as man and now..." She gestured at his naked body. "Now we need to find you some clothes."

"I didn't do that on purpose. It just happened. Probably as a side effect of Brigid's magic."

She seemed to accept this explanation. "Okay. Are you ready to keep moving?"

After a second of surprise, he laughed. He couldn't help but admire her. She wasn't a shifter, but she'd been as fast and strong and sure as one.

"What the hell was that, back in there?" Still breathing hard, he straightened and turned to look at her. "Brigid has so much magic, she should have been able to stop us. Did she just *let* us escape? There must have been thirty thousand in there. None of them even reacted."

With a graceful shrug, Marika stretched. "Her magic backfired. I guess she can't control how broad her range is. They were all trapped by her power."

"Except for you."

Looking down, she shifted her weight from foot to foot. "Yeah."

"How? How'd you do that?"

"Honestly, I have no idea. When she started talking about Dani and capturing all the children like her, I knew I couldn't let her do that."

"The power of your convictions, eh?" He grinned at her. The rush of adrenaline pumping through his veins made him feel overcharged and restless. And horny as hell.

His body reflected this. Suddenly, his nakedness felt awkward rather than natural. He felt exposed and vulnerable.

But Marika seemed to be looking every-where besides directly at him. "I guess." She didn't sound at all enthused. When she flicked a quick glance his way, an electric shock went through him.

Already aroused, his body thickened.

Still, he managed to speak. "I think your magic is stronger than you realize."

A sudden flash of anger singed her eyes. "If that's the case, why can't I find Dani? That's all I really want. If I have power, why can't I see my daughter?"

"Our daughter," he reminded her, keeping his tone mild, willing his body to return to nor-mal. "I don't know why you can't telepathically find Dani. But then I don't know much about magic or how it works. I'm just an ordinary shape-shifter."

For a moment she stared at him, keeping her gaze firmly on his face. Finally, she gave him a wan smile.

"Well, Mr. Ordinary Shifter, now what? Where do we go from here? No one seems to know where the children are."

"We've got to keep moving, keep looking for them. We'll need to get a car." He started walking, heading down toward another ribbon of road visible below them. He'd rather expose his naked backside to her than his aroused front, especially since they'd both done a great job of pretending not to notice it.

No sound. Was she following? A quick glance over his shoulder revealed that she was still standing, as though she couldn't make up her mind.

"Come on. She can't control them forever. Eventually, all those people will break out of Brigid's spell. We don't want to be anywhere near here when they do."

She blinked, then after a moment, nodded. "I'm coming. But I've gotta tell you, I don't like this. At all. I'm a Huntress, Beck. I hunt, I don't flee."

This he could identify with. He also found it reckless. "You want to stay and try to fight all of them? There's two of us, and I'm stark naked. There must have been several thousand of both vamps and shifters."

She caught up with him, grabbing his arm. "If I thought for a moment that Brigid— or any of them—knew how to find Dani, I would risk it."

"Me, too," he said, meaning it. "But they aren't any closer to knowing that than we are. We've got to stay one step ahead of them."

"You don't find this ridiculous? You and I, elite fighters among our kind, running from a fight with no idea what to do next?"

"Of course I do." He snarled, revealing his frustration. "I'm aggravated as hell. The only thing we've got to go on is the fact that Dani— and the other kids—are trying to communicate."

"Brigid knows I wouldn't willingly help her find my daughter."

"For Dani's sake, if it meant her safety, I think you'd do just about anything. I know I would."

Since he was right, she said nothing at first. Then she said, "If you can hear Dani, you should try again to communicate. Maybe she can tell us where she is."

"It's worth a shot." He hid his doubt with a smile.

"Try now." Slipping her hand into his, she gazed up at him. "Please."

Dutifully he closed his eyes, trying to still his rapid heartbeat, and let the silence fill him.

Then he sent his thoughts out, seeking, searching. "Dani?" Calling to her with his mind.

"Find me." The childish demand startled him. "You and Mama come here. Now."

And then, before he could question her, she was gone.

Reluctantly he opened his eyes. "I heard her," he said, still amazed. "She didn't sound hurt or upset or even tired."

Marika gripped his hand so hard it hurt. "How did she sound? What did she say?"

"Find me."

Appearing stunned, she stared. "That's all?"

"Yes." He gave her a hard look, his determination strengthened by his little girl's demand. "And that's exactly what we're going to do."

"How?"

"We'll go to Alpine. Addie has a sister named Annabelle who lives there. Maybe she's heard from Addie. I don't know why I didn't think of her earlier. It's a long shot, but it's better than nothing."

They headed for the road. Once they'd reached blacktop, they kept to the edge, skirting the fringes of the trees, ready to fade into the shadows at the first sign of pursuit.

At the first house they came to, they kicked in the back door. Raiding the closet, Beck found a pair of jeans that fit, albeit loosely, and a T-shirt. Once he'd dressed, they stole a silver Mustang from the driveway. He hot-wired it, and soon they were on the move again, heading northeast.

Even though they still had no inkling where Dani was being held and they could search every house between here and the border, it would be like trying to find a needle in a haystack. At least Addie's sister would be a place to start. If Brigid hadn't gotten to her first.

When he voiced these thoughts, Marika nodded in agreement.

He glanced at her as they drove. "Have you ever trusted Brigid? You must have, to have believed her warning about shifters."

"She was right about that. Shifters have Dani."

"Again, you don't know that. And, even if they do, they might be trying to protect her from Brigid. Answer my question. Have you ever trusted Brigid?"

"I—" Looking away, she didn't continue.

"You don't. You don't trust her," he answered

his own question, satisfied. "If you did, you wouldn't have been on the run with Dani in the first place. You would have let Brigid take you under her wing and use her powers to protect you both."

"That has nothing to do with me trusting Brigid." She glared at him. "Dani doesn't like her."

"Smart kid," he shot back.

"Maybe." She tossed him a half smile. "I do trust her instincts."

For the first time, he began to have an inkling what Marika's life had been like since she'd gotten pregnant with Dani. Always on the run, unsure of who to trust, not knowing if the next person she met would be her friend or a mortal enemy.

"You know…" She glanced sideways at him. "Maybe you could try one more time to hear her voice."

He stared at the road ahead of them, wondering if he should admit the truth. "She asked us to find her."

"Then see if she can at least tell you if we're heading in the right direction."

With a nod and keeping his eyes on the road,

he tried to send his thoughts out again, seeking Dani. This time, there was no connection, only the sound of the car engine and the tires on the pavement.

"Nothing," he finally said. "I'm sorry."

"At least you tried."

"I think she has to initiate it. Both times she was calling out. It's her, not me. I have no powers, no magical ability to locate a small child."

She'd turned away so he couldn't see her expression. "Maybe your connection is through blood. Yours and hers. The same."

Then she looked at him. The naked longing in her eyes was his undoing. At that moment, he wished more than anything he had the ability to do what she asked.

"Please. I want you to try every hour to contact our daughter."

Our daughter. The words, her closeness, even without scent, made him dizzy. Despite her careful avoidance earlier of his nakedness, he wondered if she knew how badly he wanted her. Even now, despite everything. He was much safer if she remained oblivious—Marika wouldn't be above using his desire to her own advantage, especially if it came to Dani.

Leaving her hand on his shoulder, he felt her touch burning through his thin cotton T-shirt.

"Marika, you heard Brigid in there. You should be able to contact Dani, if you let your magic help you."

"Sounds good in theory, but I don't know how."

"I don't know how, either," he told her sadly. "Both times, she broadcast herself over the wind. I was able to simply listen and hear her."

"What about now? Try to make out the sound of her voice. Maybe she's still calling out and you haven't been trying to hear her."

Though he knew Dani was silent—last time there'd been no mistaking the frustration in her young voice—he nodded.

"Thank you." She brushed a quick kiss against his cheek, making him dizzy. "I need to know she's all right."

He fought the urge to reach up and touch the spot where she'd kissed him. Put that way, with her huge eyes full of liquid worry, he had no choice but to agree.

He pulled off the main road onto a dirt track that wound through empty prairie and parked.

Then, avoiding her gaze, he got out of the car. A second later, she followed.

Closing his eyes to remove the distraction of Marika's face, he tried tentatively to send tendrils of thought out into the universe.

Nothing. But then, what had he expected? He could change from human to wolf, he could fight, was an expert marksman and sniper, but magic wasn't his thing. He'd bet Marika had more power in her index finger than he had in his entire body.

Still, because he already wholeheartedly loved this tiny daughter he'd never even met, he tried yet again, putting every fiber of his being into the sending. He longed—how he wanted—to once again hear her little high-pitched voice calling out a childish demand. Even more, he'd have loved to see her precious baby face, to breathe the scent of her skin, and hold her close.

His daughter. His. Dani.

He waited, throwing himself out there again, into nothing, into everything, not sure exactly how such a thing should be done and hoping he was doing it right.

Silence.

As the minutes ticked by and nothing happened, he became suspicious that his best effort might not be enough. He could fight, he could hunt, and being a Protector had taught him many other skills over the years, but he couldn't contact one little girl.

Beck despised failure. Since his teenager years, he'd taken steps to ensure success. No matter what it took, no matter how hard the struggle, he would prevail.

So here he stood, listening to the wind, struggling to hear a tiny cry, desperately trying, and…nothing.

Nothing. Completely unacceptable. Experience had taught him if he tried hard enough, he'd achieve results.

Yet he heard only silence.

Come on, he railed silently. Give me something, he cursed, without moving his mouth. He had no magic, yet still, he dared to hope for something. Something, anything. For Marika's sake. And his.

Instead, he got nothing. That, and the steady drumming of his heartbeat in his ears.

Damn. Hope shriveled up inside his chest. Praying his daughter was still alive, he felt like a complete and utter failure. Worse, he had to open his eyes, look the woman he loved in the face and tell her he hadn't succeeded.

The woman he loved? He sucked in his breath, shocked. Whoa! Where had that come from?

Rattled and hating that he'd allowed himself to become so distracted, he worked hard to slow his racing heart and even out his breathing before he gave Marika the bad news.

Then, just as he was about to concede defeat, to shut down his mind and heart and soul, he heard the softest sound, a whisper only, calling a name.

Mama.

He froze, unable to breathe. It was her. Dani. This time, crying for her mother instead of demanding he find her.

Dani. Awkwardly, he tried to comfort her with his mind. She didn't even know him, and in his isolated former life as a Protector, he'd had zero experience with children, especially one so small. But she was his, his daughter, his baby, his child, his own flesh and blood. He loved her without even meeting her. Loved her with a desperation that both humbled and empowered him. He'd do anything for her.

"Anything, baby girl," he said out loud.

Using every ounce of his strength, he tried to impart all that love to her, hoping she could relate to that emotion, even though to her he was only a stranger.

Her daddy.

When he finally connected to her, mind to mind, he felt surprise, then a child's innocent curiosity.

Bad man?

"No," he assured her. "A friend."

Silence while she considered this. Then, *Find me. Want Mama.*

"She's right here, with me."

Apparently not believing him, she began to wail, crying for her mother over and over, the cry becoming a scream, then a shriek.

Beck struggled against her pain, fighting the urge to double over and cover his ears.

"I. Want. Mama."

In response, the wind picked up, gusting fiercely, sending leaves and dirt spinning around them.

"Dani?" Marika cried out, letting his shoulder go and spinning in a slow circle. From the desperation on her face, he knew she couldn't hear. Anguish deepened her voice. "Dani, it's Mommy. Where are you, honey?"

He listened for another sound, another cry, anything. But even as the wind died as quickly as it had come, he knew. Dani was gone. His limited contact with their child had vanished.

But still, he'd been able to reach her. And having done so once, maybe he could do it again.

"What happened?" Leaning in close and peering into his face, Marika clutched at him, his T-shirt bunched in her fists.

"She didn't—" he began.

But she didn't want to hear that. "No. I know you heard her. I can feel it in my bones. I want to know what she said, what she's doing, how she is. Please. Tell me."

Though he knew the truth would hurt her, he couldn't lie. "She's only two. All she said was *mama*. Though she did ask me if I was a bad man."

Fist against her mouth, Marika nodded. Tears rolled unchecked down her perfect cheeks. "Nothing else?" she managed to ask. "She didn't give you a clue where she is?"

"No."

She made a sound, part sob, part groan.

Consequences be damned. Chest aching, he pulled her to him. "Shh," he whispered into her hair. Gently, he wiped away her tears. "We'll find her, she'll be all right, I—"

Raising her face to his, she parted her beautiful lips. "Kiss me," she demanded. "Kiss me and give me your mind. I want to see what you saw, hear what you heard."

"If I only could," he began, only to be silenced by her mouth on his.

"If you can't do that, then banish this pain," she murmured.

Though he knew he should resist—she wanted him for all the wrong reasons—the temptation of her moist mouth proved too much. He claimed her lips, devouring her softness. Savagely, she kissed him back, her hands caressing him, making new demands without saying a word.

Ah, desire, slamming into him, roared through his aroused body, insisting he take her here and now and hard and fast and deep.

But no. He fought himself and her. If this was the way it was going to be, he refused to let her take control. Though his blood pounded in his ears, and her skillful touch had him on fire, deliberately he slowed things down.

Slowly, he let himself taste her, moving from her mouth to her skin, kissing the tip of her nose, her salty tears, and finally trailing a path down her neck to the hollow in the base of her throat.

She shuddered and moved against him, urging him with her body. The animal inside him snarled, restless. Beck fought both himself and her, his desire and animalistic nature at odds with his mind. In this he would not be hurried. He'd wanted her too long.

Another startling truth and one he wouldn't dwell on now. Hell, he could barely even think coherently with her lush body pressed seductively against him.

He let himself touch her, sliding his hand across her silken belly, catching his breath when she writhed against him, inviting more. And hounds help him, he wanted more.

Slowly, slowly. Difficult, even excruciating,

when every instinct urged him to take her now. Right now.

She stroked his arousal. Body straining at her touch, he grunted, catching her hand. "No," he managed. "We do this my way or not at all."

Eyes dark with desire, she stared at him, finally nodding. Then, he slid his hand down the curve of her back. She caught her breath in an audible hiss. She arched toward him, to him, tempting, so tempting.

Yet he resisted, using a strength of will he hadn't even been aware he possessed. One glance at her, and he burned. Marika, pale skin gleaming like cream in the late-afternoon light, shivering with desire at his touch. Her perfect shape taunted him. Never had he craved anything, anyone so badly. Every instinct, ever nerve and pore and cell urged him to make love to her, to find that remembered pleasure in her body, again and again and again. Now.

Still, one single step from redemption, he held back. Perversely, he needed more. "Marika, stop."

She looked up at him, her eyes heavy-lidded with desire. "What?"

"I don't want to be your escape from harsh

reality or an entertaining way to blow off steam."

"Then what do you want?" she cried, her voice echoing her frustration.

"I want it all. I want you mindless and quivering, burning for me, as desperate to feel me inside you as I am to be there," he growled. "I want to be the center of your universe, if only for this moment, as vital to your survival as you are to mine."

She went still, her gaze searching his. "That sounds like you want me to be your mate."

Mate. That word again. Over the years, the word and Marika had become synonymous, though he'd buried the thought deep inside his psyche.

"Don't do this to me," she cried. "I can't handle this right now. Our little girl is missing."

She was right. He shared her pain.

"Later, then," he promised, and kissed her, shoving aside his aching heart so he could be what she wanted, what she needed.

Mindless passion. Maybe that's what they both needed.

Kissing her deeply, he felt the restlessness

inside him go quiet as she gave herself over to him.

So he took his time, making his touch both gentle and rough, exploring her body with his hands. Her nipples, taut beneath the soft cloth of her T-shirt, begged for his touch, his mouth.

She moaned, groaned, writhed beneath his touch. He knew how to stroke her, remembered where she liked to be touched. Head back, her eyes heavy-lidded with desire, she called his name in a broken whisper, pleading.

When her small hand closed around him, already aroused to the point of exploding, he knew he could resist no longer.

This time, when she slid her hands under his T-shirt, he helped her lift it. They both removed their clothes, both helping and hindering each other in their eagerness.

Finally, when she was naked, he took a moment to drink in the perfection of her lush, sensual body, before crushing her to him and claiming her mouth again.

This time, his kiss was urgent, hungry. And she kissed him back with a demanding eagerness that seared him.

When she climbed across his body to straddle him, he helped her, marveling at how her skin felt like both fire and ice. Then she slid her center down over him, burying him deep inside her, and he forgot how to think about anything else but her.

Marika. Her name on his lips, echoing with each beat of his heart, with each thrust of his body. Marika. Marika. His. Only his. His Mate.

She gasped, her body clenching around him. Sweet agony. He held himself back as long as he could, his soul tearing apart piece by piece until finally, he gave himself over to sensation and shattered.

He held her while their breathing quieted and his heartbeat returned to normal. Held her as if oblivion would stay with them, aware in the corner of his mind that they couldn't escape forever.

Still, they clutched each other close, taking pleasure, taking comfort when they could, not knowing when or if they'd get to do so again.

Meanwhile, inside, his wolf clamored to break free. Sex and strong emotions did that sometimes. "I need a few minutes to change," he told her. "My wolf needs a break."

"Go." She waved him away. "I need some

time alone to think anyway before we get back
on the road."

As soon as he reached the first twisted set
of trees, he shed his clothes, dropped to the
ground and let the change rip through him.

The instant he became wolf, he took off running. He ran like the hounds of hell chased
him, ran as if he could escape the past three
years, part of him wishing he could stay wolf
forever. Animals were free of complicated
emotions and fears. They hunted, ate and slept
and, when they woke, did it all over again. This
wasn't the first time he'd identified with those
the Pack called Ferals and it would no doubt
not be the last.

Finally, he killed a wild hare and ate, using a
small, running stream to wash the blood from
his fur.

Then, exhausted, he padded back to the spot
where he'd left his clothing. Changing back to
human, he dressed silently, wishing his changing to wolf had been able to ease the knot in
his stomach.

Man again, he still had to face what he'd
done.

Now what? Dragging his hands through his

hair for what felt like the hundredth time, he mentally gave himself a kick in the butt. Stupid, stupid, stupid. Things were complicated enough. What had he been thinking, making love to Marika?

Thinking? Right. Problem was, neither of them had been doing much rational thinking at the time.

Returning, he found Marika where he'd left her. As he walked up to her, the cell phone rang. He didn't recognize the number showing in caller ID.

Opening it, he struggled to sound normal as he said hello.

It was Brigid.

"What do you want?" he snarled, every fiber of his being going on instant alert.

"I've had a vision and I now know where Dani is," she said. "If you want to find her, you'll do exactly as I say."

Chapter 10

Stretching languidly, Marika watched rage flash across Beck's chiseled face as he listened for what seemed like an eternity.

"Go to hell," he finally said, then closed the phone, disconnecting the call.

"That was Brigid," he said. "She claims to know where we can find Dani."

Though instant hope leaped inside her at his words, she shared his skepticism. "Now she suddenly knows? How?"

"She claims to have had a vision."

"Since the gathering? If that's true, why'd she only talk to you? You'd think she'd ask for me."

His gaze searched her face. "Could you sense if she was lying?"

Sitting up, she lifted one shoulder. "Who knows. I'm not as certain that I have as much magical ability as you think I have. What did she want us to do?"

"That's just it. She's still playing games. She also said she has Addie's sister, so she told me not to waste time going to Alpine. She wants us to go back to her temple."

"She doesn't want us to go to Alpine. There must be a reason."

"Yeah. And she knew we'd talked to Dani."

Marika gasped. "How?"

"I don't know. She must be able to tap into it somehow."

"No." She got to her feet, her naked body a glorious sight. "She can't. If she could, she wouldn't need to capture the parents. Come on, let's get going. Let's get to Alpine before she does, assuming she hasn't gotten Addie's sister yet."

"I agree." Silently, she dressed. As they walked back to the truck and got in, he asked the question that had been on his mind since they'd made love. "Do you think anything will come of this?"

"Come of...you mean, of us making love?"

"Having sex," he corrected. "Yes, that's what I meant."

His insistence on changing the phrase was telling. Three years ago, he'd been the one who'd insisted on keeping things casual. Now, without actually saying the words, he was telling her not to take things too seriously. She supposed she couldn't blame him. After all, she'd kept the existence of their child secret from him for two years.

"Are you worried I'll get pregnant again?"

He shot her a glance. "Are you?"

Forcing a laugh, she shook her head. "No. I'm a vampire. I think that what happened before was a once-in-a-lifetime opportunity."

"Do you? Biology being what it is, if it happened once, it can happen again. I think we'd be foolish to think otherwise."

The thought of another child with Beck made her dizzy. She took a deep breath, willing her voice steady. "True, I guess. If we, er, do that again, maybe you'd better use protection."

He lifted a brow but didn't comment.

"Oh, and Beck, about the other," she rushed on, feeling slightly foolish. "Don't worry. Just because I said we made love doesn't mean I suddenly think I'm in love with you."

He blinked. "I wasn't worried." He sounded supremely confident. "I know you, even after all this time apart. You're like me. You don't believe there's any such animal."

Again he'd managed to shock her. "You don't believe in love?"

"Nope."

"You've never been in love, not even once?"

An inelegant snort escaped him. "No. I told you, I don't believe in it."

He was lying. She knew it in her bones. And, though she also knew she should leave it alone, she persisted. "Juliet told me all shifters have a mate. It's just a matter of finding the right one. Maybe you haven't met her yet." As she spoke, she felt a pang of grief at the idea that someone else could be his mate.

"Soul mates? So they say."

"Is that a note of cynicism?"

"Definitely," he said, unapologetic.

Falling silent, she listened to the faint sound of him breathing, wishing she could find the right words. But then, he'd think she was a fool. Hell, maybe she was.

"What about you?" he asked. "Have you ever been in love?"

In love. Suddenly flustered, she looked down at her hands. "You have to realize, I've been alive for centuries."

"Are you stalling?"

"Maybe."

He flashed a grin, dazzling her. "It's okay. I'm sure there must have been several over the years."

Several? She'd believed herself in love many times, and when she tried to remember their faces, all she could see was one man. Beck. She'd never met anyone who made her feel the way he did. Nor would she now. He was the father of her child.

The silence stretched out while she pondered.

"Answer the question."

"I've thought I was in love, yes." With him.

His expression was suddenly serious. "Then what happened?"

"Life got in the way."

Realizing that, for whatever reason, how she

answered was important to him, she thought long and hard about the rest of what she'd say. There wasn't any way he'd realize she was talking about him. "We went our separate ways. I think we always sort of thought we'd get back together, but it never happened."

He nodded, then concentrated on the road.

"Brigid's dangerous," he said, changing the subject. "You need to understand that. Whether you perceive her as a threat or not is beside the point. After that scene back there at her meeting, there's no way we can even remotely believe she wants to help us."

Swallowing, she pushed away the hurt. Forcing herself to return to reality was necessary. "I did warn you."

"You did." He gave a grim nod. "But this is more than that. I'm not sure what happened, why she told you that she couldn't train you, but you had the power to deflect her spell."

Since she couldn't disagree with this, she nodded. "I'm not sure how I did that, but it worked out."

"And Brigid will not have liked it. I think she's running scared, afraid of losing the iron grip she seems to have over all the vamps. I don't think she's ever come up against someone with as much power as you before."

Here he went again. She sighed. "Beck, while I'd love to believe I'm some superpowerful vampire witch, I'm not. Brigid herself did the assessment. I came out subpar on all categories. I had so little magical strength that she couldn't train me."

Though the words were painful, she went on. "That was a moment of great shame to me. Brigid rarely refuses anyone."

"Surely you must consider that Brigid wasn't telling the truth. Especially now. I saw what you can do. If you feel like you have to hide it, then fine, but not from me."

"There's nothing to hide. At least that I know of." He'd given her much to think about.

"Right." He glanced at her. His dark gaze searched her face, sending a frisson of pleasure through her before he returned his attention to driving. "Marika, from now on, I don't want there to be any secrets between us, okay?"

Thinking of her feelings for him, emotions that had never really vanished but now grew stronger every second they spent together, she knew she shouldn't agree.

"Okay," she said and nodded. "No secrets."

A yellow road sign flashed past. Alpine, twenty miles. One of the things she loved about this area was the way the burnt grasslands seemed to stretch on forever. And the complete and utter lack of traffic on the wide, well-maintained road.

Just when she thought the silence had grown comfortable, he broke it.

"You know," he said, his casual tone at war with his serious expression, "when you vanished right after Juliet was killed, I couldn't help but wonder if you had something to do with her death."

Shocked and momentarily speechless, she could only stare. "You knew me, know me. How could you even say such a thing?"

"I thought I knew you, but then you were gone." A shadow crossed his face. "You were the one person who understood how I felt, the single other who might have been able to grieve as intensely as I did. I thought we were…close."

"We were," she protested, heart sinking.

His hard stare never wavered from the road. "But you disappeared. No message, nothing. You didn't even send flowers to her funeral, for hounds' sake. It was almost as if, as far as you were concerned, Juliet never existed."

Though she deserved them, his words cut her deeply.

No secrets.

"I wanted to go to Juliet's funeral. I intended to, actually, but I was busy trying to stay alive. The night Juliet was murdered, when we separated and you went to the bar to meet her, someone broke into our room and tried to kill me."

He went very still, his eyes narrow. "You've never mentioned this before."

"No." She gave a self-deprecating laugh. "It was another reason to be wary of everyone. Plus, I didn't think you'd believe me. I mean, come on. Why would anyone want to kill me? At first, I thought it was because we'd broken the big taboo and had an interracial relationship."

"They're not expressly forbidden," he protested, steering them smoothly around a wide curve.

"No, but they're not looked upon favorably, either. You know that as well as I do."

"Still, that doesn't explain why you thought I wouldn't believe you."

No lies.

"When I learned I was pregnant, I didn't know how to face you, what I'd say."

"Then after you'd had our baby, you were too busy avoiding me." Bitterness colored his voice.

"Yes." Amazing how much truth hurt. Taking a deep breath, she continued. "Even if I had gotten the courage to find you, to tell you about Dani, I didn't think you'd believe me. Or, quite frankly, give a damn. After all I'd done to you—disappearing, birthing our child and raising her without you knowing—I didn't think you'd care."

Holding her breath, she waited for his reply. And waited. And waited.

Finally, he nodded. "Fair enough. Now, tell me what happened."

Ignoring the ache inside her, she answered as best she could. "That night, after we made love, you went to Addie's Bar to meet Juliet, and I took a shower in our hotel room."

He nodded, his expression emotionless.

"Someone broke into the room. They were

waiting for me when I got out of the shower. I fought him, naked. At first, I thought he wanted to rape me."

"Shifter? Or vampire?"

"Neither. The intruder was human. And, once he began struggling with me, it was plain he hadn't been told I was a vampire."

"You killed him?" Toneless, he spoke without inflection.

"No. As odd as it sounds now, I let him live. I drank enough of his blood to satisfy me, and then I let him go."

Now she saw she'd shocked him. "You made another vampire?"

"Yes." She nodded. "He couldn't hurt me, his maker. I never saw him again. So I don't know what became of him."

"Why? Why'd you set him free? He tried to kill you."

Hesitating, she studied her hands.

"Tell the truth," he urged her. "I'm trying to understand."

"I don't know if you will." Lifting her head, she straightened her shoulders. "After what we'd shared that night, I didn't want a human's death on my conscience. Killing him would have sullied our lovemaking somehow. So I fed, then I let him go."

"Just like that. You turned him and let him go."

"Yes."

His dark gaze searched her face. "Then what happened? How did you learn of Juliet's death?"

"When you didn't return, I called her cell."

He went very still. "That cell phone disappeared when she died. No one has ever been able to find it. Who answered?"

"I don't know. A man. He's the one who told me, and he laughed when he did. 'Juliet is dead,' he said." Remembered fury and pain clogged her throat. "He laughed, Beck. As if Juliet's death was the funniest thing he'd ever heard. I knew then I'd find him and kill him."

"You should have come to me. Let me help you."

"I intended to. But I'm a Huntress, remember. It's what I do. So first, I went hunting."

"And then?" His cold voice matched the chill in his eyes. "Did you find him?"

"I searched for two months without pause, stopping only to feed. Finally, I realized with so little to go on, I needed the help of someone more powerful than me. I went to Brigid, asked for her assistance. Instead, she questioned me about my pregnancy."

"Brigid knew? Did you tell her?"

"No." She bit her lip. How to explain what she'd felt, finally sharing the news with one of her own kind? The absolute shock had given way, finally, to joy. For the first time in hundreds of years, she'd felt blissfully alive. Finally fulfilled as a woman.

She was to be a mother, to carry a child in a womb that should have been dead, to nourish it through her own blood, her own body.

A vampire carrying a living child. Hope had blossomed inside her, a miracle on a par with a virgin birth. She'd quietly rejoiced, and uncertain who to trust, who to turn to, she'd trusted no one. No one would have believed her anyway.

The only thing ruining this complete and utter happiness were the two loose ends.

"Brigid helped me find the man who'd killed Juliet. We ripped him apart limb by limb."

He went still. "Are you sure? Absolutely,

without a shadow of a doubt, positive you got the right man?"

This gave her pause. "I went by what Brigid told me," she finally said. "I was certain then. Now, I'm not so sure."

Another silence fell while he digested this. Then, he raised his head and gave her a look so intent, so piercing, she gasped.

"How do you feel about possibly tearing an innocent man apart limb by limb?"

He'd asked for honesty, so she gave him that. "It's haunted me for a long time. It probably always will."

"Still, why'd you never try to find me?"

"I did," she told him, her voice steady. "But Addie said you'd gone underground because of a dispute with the Protectors."

"That didn't last forever."

"I know. Addie'd promised to notify me when you resurfaced. But before she could, Brigid warned me about you. She claimed to have seen a vision of you killing Dani."

"And you believed her?" His tone harsh, he glared at her. "You actually believed her?"

"Yes." Bowing her head, she felt ashamed. "I had no reason to doubt her." Though she ached for his arms around her, this time, he made no move to comfort her, not even a hand on her knee.

When she finally composed herself, Marika finished, telling her story in a voice as flat and emotionless as his had been earlier.

"As my condition began to show, I went into hiding. Brigid warned me against everyone. It hadn't taken long for my initial giddy happiness to be replaced by worry, terror and suspicion."

Haltingly, she told him of the poisonous words Brigid had used. She'd painted a clear picture, using the fears of a woman who'd never thought she'd ever be a mother, to make her afraid of everything and everyone around her.

"She was isolating you. I think even then, she meant to get her hands on the baby."

She glanced up at him through her lashes. The tenderness she saw in his face stunned her.

"I was so naive, so trusting. Because her vision had led her to the truth of my pregnancy, I trusted what else she told me she'd seen."

"She duped you, Marika."

"I was a fool. I can see that now. But I was so stunned by the miracle of my pregnancy,

I believed her and let her help me." When all along, she could have found Beck and had their child with him by her side. How much they'd both lost because of Brigid's poisonous lies.

Eyes filling with tears, she turned away, covering her face with her hands, alone in her pain.

He pulled the truck over to the side of the road and pulled her into his arms. He simply held her, smoothing her hair and murmuring sounds of comfort.

Then he spoke four words that made the tears start anew. *"You're no longer alone."*

As she struggled for composure, she knew a sense of overwhelming gratitude for the fact that fate had seen fit to bring them back together. Relief that this man, Anton Beck, had been the one to father her daughter—correction, *their* daughter.

And, even though she hadn't told him everything yet, for the first time since she'd learned Dani had been taken, Marika felt hope.

As he held the woman he'd once believed was his mate, Beck realized he still didn't have all the answers he needed.

"But you got away from Brigid, obviously. When and how?"

Sniffling, she gave him a watery smile and wiped at her still-streaming eyes with the back of her hand. "Brigid had business in Europe. She left me with a member of her inner circle, believing my trust and respect for her was so strong that I'd never leave. And I probably wouldn't have, had not her lieutenant made clear his contempt for me."

"Because you were pregnant?"

"Not just that, but because I carried a mixed-race child. I'd sullied my vampire blood, mixing it with that of a shifter." She gave him a sideways glance, full of concern. "He called you a dog."

"I've been called worse," he said mildly. "Did he attempt to hurt you?"

"Not directly. I think he was too afraid of Brigid for that. But he tried to make me hurt myself, to harm my own baby." Fury and disbelief mingled in her voice. "But his magic wasn't strong enough. No magic is strong enough to make me do that."

"How? Did he use spells against you?"

"I think so. He hammered at me with words, too, and tried to use his own kind of logic to convince me. I realized then that many vampires—no, most vampires—would never accept my baby, our baby. So I ran. From all of them. I went into hiding and even Brigid couldn't find me."

"How did you escape? Even with him badgering you, using his magic, you were still able to flee?"

She lifted her chin, a flash of pride shining in her eyes. "I convinced him that I believed the truth of his words, that he was right, that his magic had worked on me. I told him I needed privacy to make myself abort. Fool that he was, he believed me. He let me go into the mountains alone."

"See, I told you that you have strong magic."

"Whatever. He let me go and I ran."

"I'm sure Brigid dealt with him harshly."

"No doubt." This definitely didn't trouble her. "And even though I didn't know if he was working on behalf of Brigid or just a maniac who happened to be in her employ, because even Brigid couldn't keep me safe, I made sure I stayed hidden."

"She couldn't use her magic to find you? Maybe this Brigid isn't as powerful as she made it seem."

"No. Just like she can't use her magic to find Dani." She frowned, looking thoughtful. "And therein lies the flaw of your theory. If Brigid *is* the one after Dani, then she has many allies. Why would she need us or Addie's sister to use against us?"

"Unless…" He swallowed. If they were to no longer hide the truth, he had to throw at her any and all possibilities. "Unless Addie and Dani somehow escaped."

She pressed her lips together. "Do you think that's possible?"

"Why else would Brigid still be searching for them? I mean, if she captured them in the first place, she already knows where they are, right?"

"What about all the other children? Especially the one who they captured with the parents?"

"Again, we only have Brigid's word on that. There's no proof that these other children even exist."

Their gazes locked. He saw the moment she realized the truth. "She's playing us?"

Before he could respond, she answered herself.

"Of course she is." Anger vibrated in her voice. "That's how she operates. Nothing is ever straightforward. It's all games and lies."

He waited, knowing the larger implication would sink in eventually.

A second later her eyes widened. "But that would mean Dani is…"

"Safe." He took her hand. "But on the run, trying to hide from everyone who's trying to find her. And since Brigid has her own small army, that's a lot of vampires."

"Not to mention shifters," she responded, squeezing his hand hard. "That's the one flaw. This theory with Brigid as the bad guy doesn't account for the involvement of so many shifters."

"Actually, it does. I've said before that they might be trying to help Dani, to keep her from Brigid."

Marika nodded. "Either way, we've got to find them."

He pulled out his cell. "We're nearly at Alpine. Let me give Addie's sister a call on the off chance Brigid was lying about capturing her."

Punching in the phone number, he listened for a moment before closing the phone. "No answer. But I know where she lives. We'll just drop in on her unannounced."

He put the truck in Drive, and they pulled back out onto the road. A few minutes later, they reached the outskirts of Alpine. He turned into a residential area, then onto a dead-end street. The houses at the end backed up to the endless grasslands of the high desert.

They pulled up in front of an unassuming frame house that had been painted the same khaki color as the dried lawn.

Killing the engine, he sniffed the air. "Something's wrong."

"I sense it, too." Slowly, she got out of the truck, studying the house. "Nothing looks out of place. I'll go around back while you ring the doorbell."

But before she could even start, a woman came out of the pink stucco house next door.

"Are you looking for Annabelle?" The short Hispanic woman walked over, studying them with bright eyes. "You're the second group of people to come here in as many days. But you're too late. Annabelle passed away two weeks ago. What's really weird is that we couldn't find her sister, Addie, even to come to the funeral."

"Really." Beck and Marika exchanged a look, no doubt thinking the same thing. Had Annabelle really died or was she now a fledgling vampire?

"Who made the arrangements then? I though Addie was the only family Annabelle had."

"She was." The woman shrugged, pushing her dark hair out of her face. "But everything had been prearranged, from the casket to the burial plot. Even the tombstone was ordered in advance."

Thanking the woman, Beck walked back to the truck, while Marika stayed behind to scope out the premises.

"Sounds like Brigid got another ally," Beck commented.

As he opened the door to get in the truck, a loud cry nearly knocked him to his knees. *Mama. Want Mama.*

Chapter 11

Without even thinking, he fired back. "Dani?"

Nice man. Where Mama?

"Here. With me. Close."

Talk to her. Want Mama. Now.

Great. Now what? One little white lie and look where it had gotten him.

Dani started to cry.

While he stuttered around, trying to send soothing words, the crying stopped as Dani apparently found her own form of comfort. *Huh? Cookie?*

Apparently she was talking to someone else, someone with her, wherever she was.

A thought occurred to him. If he could get a conversation going between Dani and her companion—Addie, maybe—he might be able to get a clue as to where she was being held.

"Is Addie with you?"

No answer. He tried again, afraid he'd lost contact. "Dani, is Addie near you?"

Finally, with all the cranky petulance of an exhausted two-year-old, she answered back. *Yup. Why?*

Heart pounding, he sent, "Ask Addie where you are."

Immediate suspicion. *Why?*

"Maybe I can bring your mama to you."

Addie! she yelled. "Man wants to know where are we?"

While he couldn't hear Addie's response, he could get Dani to repeat it.

But his daughter was ahead of him. She parroted Addie's words back to him. *She dunno. Near water tower.*

Great. Near a water tower. There was one of those in every town.

"Dani, ask her how far to town. I need the name of the town."

Want Mama. Without waiting for him to respond, she started to cry again, the anguished wail of an exhausted two-year-old.

Wishing he was able to comfort her, his stomach twisted. "Dani, Dani. If you can tell me where you are, I can bring your mama to you."

Like twisting the handle on a faucet, her tears instantly vanished. *I'm in a house.*

"Good." He kept his tone soothing. "But there are lots of houses. I need to know what city."

No city, she replied promptly. *Farm. Lots of dogs.*

"Dogs? Or wolves?"

Her childish giggle had him smiling in return. *They go arooo, arooo at the moon.*

Wolves then. Fine. What had he expected? Both Marika and Brigid said shifters had grabbed her.

"Are you okay?" he asked. "No boo-boos?"

Hungry. Want geranium. And Mama. Want Mama. Find me.

She wanted a flower? He hurried to answer before she had time to start crying again.

"I'm working on that, honey. I'll find you a geranium, and your mama is with me. But

I need your help. I'm trying to find out where you are. Ask Addie what town you're in."

Huh?

"Ask Addie."

Cold. Then she made an exaggerated sound of teeth chattering.

"Dani, please. Ask Addie where you are."

Silence again. As the silence stretched on, he told himself quiet was better than crying. As long as Dani stayed connected.

"Dani?" Soft-voiced, he tried to coax her.

"What was that?" Marika came around the truck, eyeing him curiously. "I thought I heard…"

Skidding to a stop, she stared. Disappointment showed in her expression as she faced Beck. "There's no one here. Where you talking to yourself? Or…?"

"Dani," he told her. "I was talking to Dani."

Quickly, she moved to take his arm, peering up into his face. "Is she all right?"

"Yes." He relayed the short conversation. "I don't get why she wanted a flower, though."

She gave him a sad smile. "She wanted her favorite snack, not a flower. She loves nectarines, but for some reason she calls them geraniums."

"Now it makes sense." He touched her arm lightly, offering a measure of comfort. "But you heard something. What was it?"

"An echo. Maybe your voice, maybe someone else's, I'm not sure. But not Dani's."

"Maybe you're tapping in to—"

"No." She sounded so desolate, he gathered her into his arms.

"But you heard something."

"You, speaking out loud."

"But I wasn't. The entire conversation occurred in my head, silently. If you heard voices, then you *were* tapping in."

"Do you think?" Hope blazed in her eyes, lending spots of color to her normally pale cheeks.

He kissed her then, a gentle kiss on her cheek. "More than just think. *I know.* You have strong power. I don't know why it's blocked, but it's there. You heard Dani once and you can do it again. Just give it time."

"Time? What about Dani? Where did she go?"

"I don't know. If we can just get her to give us a few more hints to help us find her."

"Then let's try to contact her again."

"We can try, but like I told you, it seems to be something she has to instigate. Let's give it a few minutes, then we'll try again. She mentioned a water tower. That's a starting point, at least."

Her long lashes swept down to cover her eyes as she considered his words. Finally, she nodded and, for the second time in as many hours, Marika wept.

Empathizing completely, he held her while she cried. For people like them, letting hope in required more than a simple act of faith. Doing so felt like major surgery, opening both body and soul, exposing everything to the capricious whim of the elements.

Since Marika was brave enough to try, he wondered if he ever would gather that much courage, or if he'd permanently remain closed off, shut down and blunted.

When her sobs finally subsided, she pushed out of his arms, avoiding his gaze. Annabelle's neighbor stared, still watching them from her front lawn.

"There's a water tower in Marfa, by the jail. We can start there."

Moving in unison, they got in the truck and headed out. Before long they were speeding down U.S. 67, skirting the beautiful Paisano Peak and Twin Peaks, on their way to Marfa.

"If we kept going south toward Presidio, we could be in Mexico in a few hours," he told her, more to break the silence than anything else.

"She's not in Mexico."

Curious, he glanced at her. "How do you know?"

"Because Dani understands Spanish. I taught her myself. She would have mimicked something, probably in Spanish, if she was surrounded by non-English speakers."

"This entire area is full of Spanish speakers," he said. "I doubt there's much difference on the other side of the border."

"True. But I really don't think she's in Mexico."

Impatient, he drummed his fingers on the steering wheel. "We've got to find her before Brigid does."

"We are still assuming Brigid is our enemy."

He sighed. "What's it going to take to convince you?"

"Look, I tend to agree with you that Brigid

has something to do with this. But I don't believe she took Dani. She wants her now, true, but she didn't kidnap her."

"What are you basing this theory on?"

"Because she's still involved. If she had Dani she wouldn't waste time messing with us. She wouldn't need to."

"Good point. So she's still hunting Dani, too. Which brings us to why."

"Why?" Marika stared at him. "What do you mean?"

"Valid points, but you're leaving out the most important one. Dani. In order for her to be valuable to Brigid, she's got to have her own kind of magic. Does she?"

Marika bit her bottom lip, considering. "If she does, it hasn't manifested itself yet. And she wouldn't know how to use it once it does. Honestly, I don't think it's that simple. If Brigid is involved, she's not acting alone. There are others."

"Maybe." He was willing to concede this point. "But think of what she did back there and you have to wonder. If others are involved, are they acting of their own free will?"

They reached Marfa, appearing on the flat

landscape like an oasis in the desert. With its squat, brick buildings and sparse trees, Marfa looked like any other dusty, small west Texas town. U.S. 67 became Highland Drive and they turned left, parking in front of the El Paisano Hotel.

"This will be a good starting point."

"Yes." She glanced out her window at the heat making shimmering waves from the parking lot. "I assume you want to walk?"

"Will the temperature bother you?"

"No. But why not use the car?"

"We can learn more on foot, talk to people, hear the sounds. Plus, my sense of smell is really strong. On foot I can utilize that. I still remember Dani's scent."

"You do?"

"Of course." As if he could ever forget his own daughter's scent. The moment he'd first smelled her, that moment of wonder and shock would stay with him forever.

They got out of the car and began walking.

Finally, after roaming Marfa for a few hours, frequenting every café and store, including El Cheapo Liquor, and describing their little girl to endless strangers, they had to admit defeat. No one came forward and claimed to have seen her.

As dusk gathered in the wide-open sky, they sat at an outdoor table at Squeeze Marfa, a small, health-conscious café across from the Presidio County courthouse, and sipped smoothies. Even though darkness had not yet descended, most of the shops had already closed, and the street was deserted. In the past ten minutes, not a single car had driven by.

Pale streamers of pink and orange streaked across the sky. A man could get used to a place like this, Beck thought. During the day he'd seen a sign that had proclaimed that the town's population, at 2,400 people, was exactly half of its altitude of 4,800 feet. It was a quirky place, built with a west Texas rancher's sensibilities. A rancher town combined with a New Age, almost California, feel.

"I like Marfa," he said, speaking his thoughts out loud.

"Me, too. I always have. But Dani's not here." Marika rested her chin on her hands, playing with her straw and stirring her smoothy.

He hated that she sounded so dejected.

Reaching across the table, he covered her hand with his. "Let's try again to contact her."

Her startled gaze flew to his. "Do you think we can? I thought you said—"

"I know what I said, that's she's always the one to initiate contact. That's true, but on the other hand, I've only tried that one time to reach her. Let's make the attempt again. Together. Maybe with your magic to boost me, we'll have better luck."

This time, she didn't protest his comments about her magic. Instead, eyes blazing, she nodded and curled her long, elegant fingers around his. "Okay. You start."

Her touch made him dizzy. Taking a deep breath, he closed his eyes. Exhaling, he sent his mind out, both concentrating and searching. Using mental imagery, he pictured an airplane, a fighter jet, speeding like a bullet into the midst of a thunderstorm, lights blinking, undaunted. A search-and-rescue mission. Hounds knew, he'd done enough of those during his career as a Protector.

"Dani?" Mentally, he shouted her name. Marika squeezed his hand, as though lending him strength.

"Dani?" He tried again.

They waited.

No response.

He tried once more, a sliver of desperation sparking his energy. "Dani?"

Nothing. Nothing but silence.

Now Marika gripped his hand so tightly it ached. The rawness of her pain transmitted to him through her touch.

"You try," he told her.

As if startled, she looked at him. "I don't know how," she admitted.

"Neither did I. Just concentrate as hard as you can." Intertwining his fingers with hers, he gave her his most reassuring smile. "Try to find her."

Swallowing, she lifted her chin. "Okay." Closing her eyes, she went absolutely, utterly still.

Unbelievably, he felt the touch of her mind as she sent out one word, one name. *Dani.*

"Dani," she whispered out loud, her voice raw. "Please answer. I love you and miss you. Where are you, baby?"

Again, only silence. But Marika refused to give up.

Over and over, she silently cried out their daughter's name, seeking, searching, until finally…

Mama! So much joy in that youthful cry.

MAMA! The childish scream echoed in their minds. *Mama, Mama, Mama! Mama, where are you?*

"Looking for you, Dani-girl." Marika blinked, visibly holding back tears. "Baby, you've got to help Mama find you, okay?"

Throat tight, Beck glanced at her, admiring how she struggled to maintain her composure, obviously not wanting her little girl to hear her break down.

"Dani, ask Addie where you are?"

Okay dokey. Addie? Mama want to know where we are.

A brief pause, while Dani clearly listened, then, *Mama, Addie says to tell you she's keeping me safe.*

Safe was good, but not enough. Beck squeezed Marika's hand. "Ask her again."

Marika nodded. "Ask Addie what town?"

Mama come. Mama come now. Dani sounded petulant. *I want you, Mama. Why won't you come?*

"I'm trying, baby girl." Marika's voice broke. A silver tear streaked its way down her cheek, splashing onto the back of Beck's hand. "But I can't get there if I can't find you."

Mama lost? Dani seemed to find this amusing. Her bright, childish laughter rang out like a perfect bell. *You funny, Mama.*

"Dani, we need to know how to get there," Beck said. "Please ask Addie and tell your mother."

Who man, Mama? Voice sounding suspicious, Dani seemed to pull back into herself. "Is he...friend?"

Sniffing, Marika struggled to regain her composure. "Yes, honey. Beck is...a friend. He's trying to help me find you."

I hide, Mommy. I hide good. Satisfaction rang in the little girl's voice. *Even the dogs can't find me.*

Marika recoiled, yanking her hand from Beck's. "The dogs? Shape-shifters?"

But Dani was gone.

Marika turned an accusing stare on him. "So much for your Brigid theory. She's being held by shape-shifters."

"You don't know that. There might actually

be dogs wherever she is. Real dogs. People do still have them, you know."

She shot him a look, letting him know she could do without the sarcasm. "Let's try again. If we can reach her again, maybe we can get directions."

He got up, dropped their empty plastic cups in the trash bin and returned to their table. "I'm ready if you are."

Expression full of hope, she closed her eyes. "Dani?"

Silently, he waited, still standing.

"Dani?" she called again, a bit louder.

No response.

He let her make several more attempts and even tried himself, silently. But this time, they didn't make it through the cosmos to their little girl.

Finally, even Marika conceded defeat. Standing, she wiped her hands on the front of her chinos and gave him a brilliant and utterly false smile. "At least we know we *can* contact her, right?"

"Apparently only when she wants to be contacted." He touched her shoulder, a light touch. "Let's see if there are any rooms available at the El Paisano. We need to regroup, take a break and try to come up with a plan."

"And try to contact Dani?"

"Of course," he replied.

The hotel had a vacancy, and, after entering the room, Marika compulsively inspected the window, the deadbolt on the door and the bathroom. The room was well-worn and clean, yet being there made her uncomfortable. She'd never been overly fond of confined spaces, but she had to agree with Beck. They needed space and solitude to see if they could get Dani to tell them where she was. Maybe this would do the trick.

Once they'd closed and locked the door, he took a quick shower, then climbed into the queen-size bed. Grinning up at her, he patted the comforter. "Sit."

Feeling oddly uncomfortable, as though she no longer fit in her own skin, Marika perched on the edge of the bed. Impatience jangled her insides, making her want to lash out, to rage, anything to feel as though she was taking action.

"This feels wrong," she complained. "Just

sitting here in an air-conditioned motel room. We should be doing something."

"We are." He gave her a wry smile. "First we're going to freshen up. Then we're going to try again to contact Dani. If she can give us any more information, something that would help us find her, we'll be able to work out a plan. This aimless driving around isn't productive."

"We're searching, at least. That's something."

"We can't search the entire state. We need to narrow it down."

Since she agreed with this, she nodded. "What now? The situation is urgent. Shouldn't we be trying to contact her?"

"We will. Settle down," he said, his voice soothing. "An hour to clear our heads isn't going to hurt anything."

"But—"

"It will help, Marika." Kneading her shoulder, he pulled her close. "I want to see what happens if I can get into a more meditative state before I contact her. Work with me."

Swallowing back a curse, she tried to relax. Not easy, when all she could think about was her baby girl calling her name.

But if he was right, if these few minutes of quiet helped, then she needed to still her nerves for his sake.

He continued to rub her shoulder and she tried, honestly tried, to relax into his touch. But she couldn't quiet her restlessness, and finally she pushed herself up off the bed.

"Go ahead and meditate," she told him. "I'm going to take a shower. That might help make me feel better."

Surprisingly, the shower helped. She made the water as hot as she could stand it, knowing when she stepped out into the air-conditioned room, she'd feel the temperature difference more drastically.

Finally she returned to the bed to see if he'd had any success in his efforts to relax. Apparently he had, since he'd fallen asleep sitting up.

Skin dark against the snowy white of the pillow, he looked both exotic and hard, beautiful and dangerous. Fleetingly, she worried that she was beginning to become obsessed with him, as she'd been during their brief time of passion. But that fear didn't keep her from wondering what he dreamed of.

Glancing at the clock, she decided to give

him one hour before waking him. She turned off the light and took a seat in the chair near the bed. As her gaze adjusted to the darkness, she felt some of her tension finally ease.

Bad clichés aside, these days she felt most at home in the dark. Sometimes, watching the enigma that Beck had become, she suspected he did, too.

After having Dani, taking care of her daughter had managed to banish the discontentment. Loving Dani had brought her a peace she'd never known.

Now, without her baby girl, she sat, knees drawn to her chest, and watched Dani's father. Aching, hoping, praying he'd be able to contact her little girl. Their little girl. And, she realized, she craved his arms around her, selfishly wanting to take what comfort his body could give.

Though the night air had grown chilly, courtesy of an impromptu cold front that had barreled in from New Mexico, he'd kicked off his blanket and lay on his side. The soft glow from the outside light highlighted his chiseled features. He alternated between looking relaxed and peaceful and tough and hard, as though he'd done and seen things that would have broken another man.

She often wondered if she looked that way, too.

Aching, wanting and worrying for no good reason that the yawning emptiness of eternal life had become too much, she finally dropped her blanket and crawled into bed beside him, telling herself she was tired of being cold and craved only to share his warmth.

Careful not to wake him, she moved closer, inch by inch, first letting her shin rest against his, then her leg, thigh and finally, upper body.

Against him, even the small scraps of cloth suddenly seemed too much. She pulled them off with a few quick motions and then rolled back into place.

When she lay skin to skin, for the first time in years, she finally felt warmth. She closed her eyes, wishing she could sleep, praying for sleep, and tried to ignore the tiny flame of desire that had sparked to life.

Occasionally, she'd glance at the clock, measuring seconds against breaths, each minute against her painstaking exploration of his body, of his skin. Of him. Beck, the father of her child, and the one she'd never managed to forget.

Then her careful touch woke him. She felt it in the change in his breathing, in the sudden swell of his arousal.

She hadn't been able to stop thinking about this, about how magnificent that part of him was, how wonderful he'd felt moving inside her. How he'd made her feel passion she'd only heard about and never thought she'd experience. How Beck made her feel, for the first time in a very long life, complete.

Again now when he touched her, she went up in flames. As his mouth covered hers, she stopped thinking completely, allowing herself to drown in a flood of sensation. Spice and heat, he smelled like sunshine, remnants of the life she'd once had, so long ago.

For a flash of an instant, she thought of the man he'd been then, before Jules had died, then pushed the image away. This was still Beck, his own man, nearly wild with desire, his masculinity hard against her belly. There was nothing hesitant about the way he touched her, and, for a split second, she envied his certainty.

Meanwhile, she kept trying to find the balance between the person she'd been and the one she was now.

Something in her thoughts must have communicated to him, as he broke off the kiss.

"Marika? Penny for them." His husky voice brought her out of her internal thoughts. He cupped her face in his hands. "Are you all right?"

"I'm fine."

"No." One corner of his sensual mouth tugged up into a half smile. "Tell me what's wrong."

"You're different," she said.

"Different? What do you mean?"

Still, she continued. "You always did everything with passion. That was one of the things that attracted me to you initially."

"Back then," he interrupted. "Right?"

"Yes, back then. You blazed through life like a volcano on the verge of erupting. You can't imagine how amazing that feels to a vampire. Our lives have a tendency to be…cold. Even though I'd lived three hundred years, I'd never met anyone like you."

Past tense. She knew he noticed that, too.

These days, except when he was touching her, he might have been the original ice man.

"And now?" He sounded harsh, like a man on the verge of strangling. "What do I seem like to you now?"

"Remote. Untouchable."

"Believe me. I'm anything but that now."

"I'm not talking about now. I mean the other times, when we're not lying naked next to each other."

"Ah, I see." He looked away, but not before she saw the shadow cross his face.

Chapter 12

"After Juliet died, and you left, I'd never felt so alone. I threw myself into my job—hell, I *lived* for my job. I decided to become the best Protector the Society had ever seen."

"Did you?"

"No." He gave her a rueful smile. "In retrospect, that's probably a good thing. My friend Simon—you met him at Brigid's earlier—was always a few steps ahead of me. Poor guy got himself known as The Terminator, because he'd exterminated so many Ferals."

"By Ferals you mean wild shifters?"

"Right. We were supposed to go assess

them, decide if they could be rehabilitated and brought back into society. The thinking was that if they were left to stay wild, they could become dangerous to humans and to others. And of course, there's always the risk they could expose the Pack."

"How many did you save?"

"At first, I tried to save all of them. But I nearly got killed twice and then I realized I had to be more objective. I began carrying out more kill orders. Eventually, I burned out."

"That must have been hard on you." She couldn't imagine what he'd felt like. Though Vampires were technically more ruthless killers than shifters, her job as a Vampire Huntress had been a bit different—she'd only destroyed the truly evil.

"You don't know the half of it. Simon was the one who realized the extent of my burn-out. He recommended me for a mandatory vacation, not knowing that was a death sentence under that particular leader. I went on the run from the very organization I'd sworn to serve."

"They hunted you?" She found this a difficult concept to follow. "Your own people?"

"Yes." In that single word, she heard a wealth

of emotion. Disgust mingled with pain, sorrow with anger. No wonder. A complex man who'd valued simple things had been forever changed by the actions of a few evil men.

No wonder Beck had changed. Who wouldn't have?

"What about you?" he asked. "Have you ever regretted becoming a Huntress?"

"No." She didn't even hesitate. "I like what I do and I'm good at it. Though I know I'll never completely stamp out evil, I get to do my part."

She lifted her chin. "Starting with the ones who took Dani."

"You know," he finally said, "searching for Dani is the only thing that gives my life purpose. Up until I found you again and learned about her, I didn't really know who I was."

Her breath caught in her chest. "What about when we find her? What then?"

He flashed her a grin so beautiful it made her chest ache to see it. "Then I'll be the best damn daddy you ever saw."

At his words, her eyes filled with tears.

"Let me help you." She touched him, resting her hand lightly on his shoulder, encouraged when he didn't move away from her. "If you'd allow me, I could help you find yourself again."

"Brave words." His mocking tone didn't match the vulnerability in his eyes. "And a big task. I'm not sure you're up for it."

She gave him her most confident smile. "I am."

Staring at her, he shook his head. "Don't expect too much. You might be disappointed."

"I doubt that."

"I don't know what you want from me."

"Beck," she said softly, keeping the rest inside, though another word played over and over in her head. *Mate.* "I want the old Beck back. Our daughter should know him. No one else."

"Not possible," he growled. "Sorry. I'll do the best I can, but there's too much water under the bridge."

She kissed him then, meaning to offer him comfort of the sweetness-and-light variety. Instead, the second their lips touched, he took over, meeting her kiss with his own, full of hunger and darkness and passion. And hope. She told herself there was always hope.

Pressing himself against her, he let her feel the strength and swell of his arousal. Her own body responded, nipples tightening as she arched her back for his touch. He cupped them, suckled them, driving her wild with need and desire. Drowning. She felt as if she was drowning.

Then he deepened the kiss, his hands boldly claiming her body, and she didn't have to speak or even think. She had only to give herself over to sensation, and the sweet, heady feel of making love with the man she cared for above all others.

Sated and refocused, Beck took a shower after their lovemaking, after which he planned to make another attempt to contact Dani. Waiting, Marika felt...restless. More than usual, as if she could jump right out of her skin.

If she'd been Pack, she would have said she needed to change, to let her inner wolf run free. Since she wasn't, she knew there was only one thing she could do, one course of action that might make her feel better.

She was a Vampire Huntress. She needed to hunt.

Slipping out from under the sheets, she padded softly to where she'd left her clothes and dressed silently. Carrying her shoes, she went to the door, hesitated, then padded over to the bathroom. Opening the door, she told him she'd be back in a few minutes.

"Hungry?" he asked. "Be careful."

She nodded. "I will be. Don't try to contact Dani without me. I'll be back before you've finished."

Outside, the desert air was crisp and cool, a welcome change from the suffocating heat of the day. The night sky looked like a velvet display dotted with well-placed diamond stars.

Suddenly ravenous, she debated whether to go left or right, then abruptly chose left. Since the hotel was situated in the center of town, she knew she wouldn't have to wander too far to find humans wandering the streets. Inebriated or otherwise, she'd take the first one she could find. She was way overdue for a long feast of fresh blood, careful to leave them alive and semiconscious, believing they'd had some kind of late-night hallucination.

Over the centuries, vampires had learned to regulate themselves if they wanted to live undetected among mankind. A set of rules had been put into place, similar to the Ten Commandments, and these rules were the first thing any fledgling vampire was taught by his or her sire.

Several of these rules addressed proper behavior when feeding from live humans. Though she was so hungry her fangs ached, Marika would be careful to obey these rules. There was too much at stake now to do something foolish and cause the humans to panic and distrust any strangers on sight.

As she'd suspected she would, less than a block from the hotel, she came across a man staggering down an alley. Tall and muscular, with work-roughened hands and sun-creased skin, his obvious state of inebriation had him unable to keep his balance. As she glided up alongside him, he struggled to focus his bleary eyes on her.

"You're a pretty one, but I'm too drunk for a hooker tonight, honey," he slurred. "Maybe look me up tomorrow afternoon. I'm staying at the Piss...Pass...Paisano."

He thought she was a prostitute. Perfect.

Giving him a coy smile, she sashayed over, slowly circling him and taking care to keep her fangs hidden.

She needn't have bothered—the man could barely focus. As he staggered around trying to watch her, she went in for the bite. Quickly, elegantly and neatly, she pierced his leathery skin, though there was nothing neat or even remotely elegant about the stench of this human who sagged against her. Nevertheless, she feasted on his delicious blood, enjoying the heady rush it gave her.

When she felt her energy levels returning to full strength, and not wanting to kill him, she judged she'd had enough and pushed herself off him. Ignoring the stench of cigarettes and alcohol and unwashed man, she was gentle as she propped him up against a trash Dumpster.

Once she'd arranged him to make it look as if he'd merely passed out, she rearranged her clothing, wiped her mouth off with the back of her hand and took a quick look at his neck.

The puncture marks left by her fangs were already closing. By the time he woke, they'd be barely noticeable. If he saw them at all, he'd probably figure some insect had gotten him. The transformation to vampire would take some time.

Mood vastly improved, Marika turned and

made her way back to the hotel, hoping Beck would be able to reach their daughter now and this time, glean some useful information.

How he'd known what Marika needed and where she was going to get it, Beck had no idea. But he had.

She was hungry and was going to feed.

The wolf side of him had no problem with that. The human side was another story.

A thousand cautions and warnings flashed through his mind in the few seconds after she'd turned away and headed toward the door. By force of will, he'd kept silent, well aware she hadn't managed to live so many centuries by being indiscreet or making foolish mistakes.

Bottom line—Marika could take care of herself.

She didn't need him to tell her how. As a matter of fact, Marika didn't really need him for anything.

Dani was another story. Two years old, his daughter needed her daddy.

Beck hadn't realized until that moment how badly he yearned to be needed. The revelation so stunned him, made him so uncomfortable, that he got up and began to pace, trying to sort out the myriad unwelcome feelings churning inside him.

He'd left the Protectors a bitter and disillusioned man, seeking only peace and solitude, believing somehow that time would heal all scars, both internal and external. Instead he'd found both passion and the tentative beginnings of hope.

Dare he allow himself to trust Marika? How could he, when she'd made it so plain she felt both she and their daughter would be better off without him?

Trust or not, in this she had no choice. He wanted to be part of his daughter's life. Would be part of her life. Like it or leave it, that wasn't going to change. Marika would have to get used to having him around.

Finally, exhausted mentally, he climbed back on top of the bed and tried to calm his churning thoughts, aware he needed to focus if he wanted to contact Dani. Thankful Marika had gone out, he tried to prepare himself.

After what seemed an eternity, she finally returned, entering the room as silently as she'd left. The first thing his sharp sense of smell detected was the bitter tang of blood, mingled with wisps of other scents—alcohol, cigarette smoke and the arid bite of human perspiration.

Having fed, her skin seemed to glow with the quiet sheen of a polished pearl. She looked both ethereal and somehow more substantial, alluring and dangerous. Seeing her, his body stirred.

Eyes glowing in the dim light, she crossed the room swiftly, climbing to sit in front of him.

Fully aroused, he wanted her so badly he shook with it, so badly he couldn't speak.

"Are you okay?" she asked, reaching for him.

He didn't answer, didn't have to. Letting his body speak for itself, he pulled her up on top of him, nestling her against his powerful erection. She gasped, then settled in close. Her clothes were in the way, and he helped her shed them, ignoring the tearing sound as he ripped off her shirt.

Once she'd removed her jeans and panties, she pushed him back and straddled him.

Sinking deep inside her was like coming

home to his own personal slice of heaven and hell, all rolled into one.

Full of fresh blood, she rode him as if she'd been gone for ages, rode him until he couldn't breathe, couldn't think, couldn't do anything but let himself go. As he filled her with his essence and held her still while she contracted around him, he knew she was the one thing he couldn't live without.

His woman. His mate.

As his breathing slowed, he continued to hold her. Miracle of miracles, she let him.

Finally, he raised his head, meaning to kiss her mouth in thanks, but something in her face stopped him.

Expression impassive, she watched him, once again motionless, looking so like a beautiful marble statue that he felt it like a physical wound. Their lovemaking had shattered his world. Had she not felt the same thing he had?

He opened his mouth to ask her and...

Mama! The shrill cry made him freeze. A quick glance at Marika and he realized she'd heard it, too.

Mama, hurry, Dani sobbed. *Bad man take Addie. She gone. Mama, I'm scared.*

"Where are you, baby?" Pushing herself to her feet, Marika spoke calmly, but Beck could hear the thread of panic under her smooth tone. "Tell Mama where you are so I can come and get you."

But the lights, Dani said, then began sobbing, her words unintelligible.

He felt a frisson of fear. His helplessness enraged him.

"The lights? What lights?"

Dani's cries became wails.

"Baby, what's happening?" Marika cried. "Where are you? Are you all right?"

But their little girl didn't answer. The sobs abruptly stopped, and the silence felt like a knife straight into his heart.

One look at Marika and he knew she felt the same.

"Come on." Stepping into his jeans, Beck hurriedly dressed. "Though it's barely dawn, people should be moving around soon. Let's get outside and check the town one more time before we get back on the road. Maybe someone knows something about lights. If not, we can try to reach Dani again later."

One step ahead of him, Marika was already

fully dressed and halfway out the door, with him close on her heels.

She came to a halt so abrupt that he nearly ran into her.

Though the wee hours of the morning were usually quiet, this time they both knew something else was amiss. The empty streets looked like something from a movie, as though giant aliens had swooped down and exterminated anything that moved. Not a single car, bus, truck or airplane disturbed the complete and utter stillness.

His uneasiness accelerated.

"There's not even a bird," she whispered, already tensing into a battle crouch. "Something's very wrong here."

"Brigid." He spoke the word like a curse. "I don't know what she did or how she did it, but I can feel the residue from her magic lingering in the air. I can feel it surrounding us, closing in."

Though she nodded, she kept moving forward.

"Marika, wait. I think we're walking into a trap."

As though he'd spoken his own form of

spell, people began to appear in the early morning streets. At first one, then two, six and then ten, they spilled from every doorway and came from around every corner. They moved in unison, with single-minded intent, their wooden steps, rigid posture and vacant stares suggesting zombies or sleepwalkers. They were obviously laboring under some kind of magical spell.

And as one, they all headed directly for Beck and Marika, moving with an unblinking intensity.

Beck and Marika exchanged a glance.

"Hellhounds," he said.

"Ditto," she snarled. "I don't know if they've been sent to capture us or kill us, but I don't intend to wait around to find out."

With that, she spun on her heel, taking off at vampire speed, with Beck right behind her.

They zigged left, then right, each time coming up short at the wall of people blocking their way. There was nowhere to run.

Around every corner, no matter which way they turned, a dead end waited. Throngs of people blocked their way.

People—all kinds. Human and vampire.

Shifters, too. All with the same vacant stare. Hundreds of them, maybe thousands. And still, more kept coming.

They were completely, utterly surrounded by a circle of Brigid's minions.

"We're going to have to fight," she said.

With anyone else, Beck would have found the odds against them astronomical. But this was Marika, and he'd seen her magic work against Brigid before.

"Use your magic," he urged. "That's the only way we stand a chance."

"I'll try." Though she didn't sound hopeful, she sounded fierce.

Back to back, each assumed battle stance. All he had was his loaded Glock and a little extra ammo. Glancing at the ever-tightening circle of people, he knew it wouldn't matter. If he shot the front line, the others would simply keep coming. There weren't enough bullets or time to take down so many.

Where her shoulder blades touched his back, he felt a tingling so strong it was a vibration, which became a gradually increasing heat. Burning. Power. Magic.

Palms up, Marika held out her hands. "Stop," she ordered.

As one, the crowd stopped. Dead in their tracks, some even with their foot raised in the act of taking another step.

As if they were under a spell.

"You used magic," he said, amazed.

"No. Yes." She held up her hands, staring at them as if she'd never seen them before. "I guess I must have. I don't know."

If she'd been anyone else, he would have suspected she was playing with him. But the wild look in her eyes told him she was serious.

"Who am I to question it? If whatever I'm doing is working, then I'll go with it." She shrugged, the slight quiver in her no-nonsense tone telling him she wasn't nearly as collected as she tried to appear.

"Try for more."

With a slight frown, she stared at him. "What?"

"My guess is that you don't know what you can do. Am I right?"

She gave a small nod.

"Then see if any of them know where Dani is. If they're under your power, you should be able to make them tell you. Or, better yet, show you."

Dipping her chin, she turned to face the nearest group. Still frozen, their expressions unchanging, they didn't even appear to realize she'd moved closer to them.

Squaring her shoulders, Marika took a deep breath. "Listen up, all of you. If anyone here knows how to find my daughter, step forward."

Not a single soul moved.

Then the group to their left parted, splitting clean down the middle like the Red Sea parting for Moses. A single woman moved among them, her walk fluid and unencumbered by the constraints of magic. Behind her trailed three others.

Renenet, the vampiress they'd feared destroyed in the house fire.

When she reached Marika, she made a slow turn, taking in the still-frozen crowd. One artfully shaped brow rose. "Brigid was afraid you'd figure out the extent of your power. I told her the stress of losing your daughter might help bring it to the forefront of your subconscious, but she wouldn't listen."

"I haven't *lost* my daughter. She was taken from me."

"Ah, you've found her then?" One corner of Renee's perfect mouth lifted, a sign of amused contempt.

Crossing her arms, Marika glared. "You know damn well I haven't. What do you want?"

"You said if anyone knew where your child was hidden, they should come forward. I might have an idea where she is, but it's plain to see I'm not wanted." She turned to go.

"Wait." Marika's soft-spoken order acted like another spell, causing the other vampire to freeze in place.

"What have you done?" All traces of amusement vanished. Instead rage and a glimmer of fear flashed across Renee's face. "Release me, this instant," she demanded. "Your magic doesn't work on me."

"Doesn't it? Where is Dani?"

"I don't know."

"You just said you did. Now tell me. Where is my little girl?"

Beck moved up to stand beside Marika, giving Renee a warning look. Behind her, her entourage clustered together, their hoods concealing their faces.

"I said I might have an idea." Renee moved her arms up slowly, grimacing as though lead weights had been tied to them. "Brigid doesn't know for sure, either, but she has had some visions of Dani and others. Something to do with the lights."

Dani had mentioned the lights. She glanced at Beck and saw comprehension flash across his face.

"The ghost lights?" Beck asked, referring to the mysterious phenomena usually seen near U.S. 67 east of Marfa.

Of course. The ghost lights.

"Yes." Fury still blazing from the other vampire's eyes, she struggled to turn herself to face him. As she moved, Beck swore he could see the bones beneath the perfect layer of creamy skin. He remembered Marika telling him that Renee was very old.

Her effort to move slowly worked. Finally, like a dog shaking off water, Renee shook herself and then faced Marika. "Brigid doesn't have your girl. She's looking for her, as well. Her and all the others like her."

"We figured that. What we don't know is why."

"I don't know. She's been looking for one like her for years. You know there are others. I think there are thirteen. Maybe more now. Even with all her power, Brigid hasn't been able to capture a single one. They might as well be dragonflies with the entire sky to fly in."

Marika's expression didn't change. "That seems odd. Do you know why? She's so powerful. How can it be that her magic doesn't work against them?"

"No one knows. Brigid herself doesn't even know. That's one of the reasons she wants so badly to capture one."

"You speak of them as if they're things, not small children." Beck moved closer, wishing he could read her expression. But when she turned her gaze on him, there was no mistaking the animosity in her eyes. He wondered where that had come from. She hadn't reacted to him like this before. Hell, she'd barely even noticed him the last—and only—time he'd seen her.

"What's it to you, shifter dog?" Her lip curled.

"As if you don't know." He ripped the words off, impatient. "I'm Dani's father."

The contempt vanished, and shock and confusion flashed across Renee's face before she managed to school her expression back to a neutral one of control. "Her father."

"You didn't know?" Marika asked, watching her closely.

"No."

"Brigid knew. I wonder why she didn't tell you."

"Because she doesn't entirely trust me," Renee admitted. "And that would explain why, when we met the last time, I was supposed to capture you both. When she wouldn't tell me why, I refused. That's why she blew up the house."

Beck and Marika exchanged a look. "*Brigid* blew up that house?"

"Oh, yeah." Renee looked disgusted. "Though she knew we wouldn't die, she wanted to punish me for what she calls 'insubordination.' But I don't work for her—never have, never will."

"Then why were you meeting with us on her behalf?"

"It sounded pretty harmless. She called in a favor and I agreed to meet with you, not capture you. The capture order came after you got there. I refused. I won't do that to one of my own kind."

"What's Brigid up to?" Marika asked, more a wondering out loud than a direct question.

Renee, however, decided to answer. "She's running scared, Marika Tarus. She's afraid of you, but more importantly, she's terrified of your daughter and the others like her."

"And you? What about you? Where do you figure in all this, and why have you come to me now?"

"Because I, like you, had a child born of another species, though mine was part Fae." Renee squared her shoulders, facing them proudly.

"Was?" Marika watched the other vampire closely. "What happened to your child?"

A flash of sorrow came and went on Renee's face. "She was in the first wave of these creatures. The shifters tried to capture her."

She shot Beck a look of hatred. "This was during the first Vampire-Pack war, many years ago. They killed her before I could save her."

Chapter 13

Renee had lost a child? Even though she'd said it was during the first Vampire-Pack war, which meant that the child had died centuries ago, her pain was still raw.

And her rage against his kind. Stunned, Beck could only watch as Marika bowed her head, touching Renenet on the arm. "I'm so sorry. You've borne your loss in secret all these years?"

"I had no choice." She lifted her chin. "Too many of our kind are distrustful of the griffon children. And even though the war is long over and we have a truce, I've never trusted them." She jabbed a finger in Beck's direction.

"But I kept hearing about more being born and realized things were preparing to shift. I could stay silent no longer. That's initially why I agreed to help Brigid. I wanted to spare other children the same fate."

Death at the hands of shifters.

Until now, Beck hadn't been entirely sure he could trust Renee. Even now, a niggle of doubt still bothered him.

Still, shifters were the ones believed to have captured Dani, though he had no proof of that, either.

Marika, however, appeared to accept what the other woman said at face value. "And now you want to help me?"

"Yes." Renee lifted her chin, meeting Beck's gaze. "Because I've seen that Brigid is no better than the shifters who are capturing these children. She only wants them so she can use them for her own gain."

Beck crossed his arms, saying nothing. He couldn't shake the creepiness of having this intimate conversation surrounded by motionless people.

As though she read his mind, Marika

glanced over at him and smiled. "Maybe we should go somewhere else and talk."

"I agree. That café is open." She pointed to a place across the street. "We might have to pour our own coffee, but at least we'll be able to sit and talk."

No one moved.

Beck shot Marika a quick look, which she returned. They both wanted to get the hell out of Marfa. But not until they heard what Renee had to say.

Seeing this, Renee sighed. "You have great magic." Renee clasped Marika's shoulder. "Crowd control. Yours is stronger than any I've seen, save Brigid's."

"Yet it didn't affect you."

"It did, but I was able to break free from your spell." Eyes twinkling, the other vampire inclined her head. "You should use your magic to find your daughter."

"We're trying," Marika said with a rueful smile. "So far we haven't had any luck."

Coughing softly, Beck tried to warn Marika not to reveal everything, not yet.

Again Renee glanced at Beck, though this time her gaze had softened. "I did not know that you are the father. You have as much to lose as Marika. I will help you, too."

He spoke for the first time. "I'm not certain we need your help."

"That's your choice." Focusing her attention back on Marika, Renee inclined her head. "Over the centuries, your name has been well respected. If you want my assistance, I will help you with what I can."

"What about Simon?" Beck asked. "The other Pack guy who was there at Brigid's little gathering? What happened to him?"

The other vampire turned her clear gaze on him. "I don't know."

Moving slowly and deliberately, Beck pulled his cell phone from his pocket, opened it and punched in the code for Simon's number. He waited while it rang and rang, and, when eventually the voice mail picked up, he disconnected the call without leaving a message.

"Still no answer," he said. "So help me, if anything's happened to him, Brigid will pay. He just got married."

"I'm sure he's fine." Marika came to him, slipping her arm around his waist. "Brigid's not in the habit of harming shifters."

"Yet," he muttered darkly. "I think we should continue to go it alone."

"I have more to say," Renee interrupted. "Will you let me speak before you make your decision?"

He shrugged, considering, then finally nodded.

Surrounding by living, breathing statues, Beck couldn't help but marvel at the surreal atmosphere. He was Pack, a shape-shifter, and had grown up balancing on the thin line between the human's narrow view of reality and the paranormal side of truth. Of course he'd known that magic existed, that elves and faeries existed in their realm of mists and enchantment, but he'd never actually seen such strong magic at work until the past few days.

Even worse, he couldn't shake the feeling he was missing something. Some clue, dangling right in front of his nose.

As Renenet continued, the words spilling from her mouth rapid-fire, his attention wandered. The elusive clue hovered just out of reach.

Something in the singsong tone of Renee's voice.

Beck needed one of those aha, flash-of-insight moments. Right now, though, they were getting nowhere.

"Renee," he interrupted, cutting off the other woman midword. "Even if we could trust you, which I doubt, why should we? What could you possibly bring to the table that we don't already have?"

"I was waiting for you to ask that." Renenet smiled. "Because I bring you this."

At her gesture, one of her hooded escorts stepped forward, opening her cloak to reveal a young boy of seven or eight years.

He stared up at them, his blue eyes huge and unafraid.

"Tell them what you told me," Renee ordered, pushing the child in front of her.

Sandy-colored hair failing over his long-lashed eyes, he offered a nervous smile, gazing at Marika. "Dani's trying to find you, you know."

Marika froze, her expression stricken. "How do you know this?" she whispered. "How do you know her name?"

"Because he was there," Renee answered for him.

Beck lifted his hand. "Let him speak for himself. How do you know Dani's looking for her mother?"

The child blinked, his smile stalling. "Because I was with her. I watched over her and some of the others, because I'm older."

Crouching down, Beck made his face level with the boy's, close enough to count his freckles. "What's your name?"

"I'm Eli."

"How old are you, Eli?"

"Eight, sir."

Beck gave him a reassuring smile. "Are you like Dani?"

Unsure, Eli frowned.

"Can you change into a griffon, too?"

Eli's eyes widened. "A griffon?"

Gentling his stern tone, Beck touched his slender shoulder. "A winged creature."

Coloring, Eli nodded. "Yes. All of us can do that."

"All of you? How many are there?"

"I don't know." With a shrug, Eli began counting, using his fingers and muttering names under his breath. "Twelve," he finally said. "Thirteen, counting me."

Thirteen. Just as Brigid had said.

"Who's holding you prisoner? Dani said something about some...dogs. Are they wolves, shape-shifters?"

Eli raised his brows, looking surprised. "No one's holding us. I thought you knew. We escaped, a week ago. We split up into two groups. Most of us wanted to go home and did."

"But you didn't?"

Eli shook his head. "No one to go home to. My family's gone. I lived in a foster home. There's nothin' there for me."

"How'd you end up here, with them?" Beck indicated the vampires.

"I've been trying to find Dani's group," the little boy explained, his expression solemn. "I've been hearing her cry a lot—she's so powerful, you know? And I've been worried."

Until now, Marika had stood stone-faced, listening. Now she came closer, dropping onto her haunches and peering intently into Eli's freckled face. "What do you mean, she's so powerful?"

His pale skin reddened. "She can send her voice way farther than any of us can. She's only a baby, but she can change quicker, fly faster and do more fancy flips and stuff than us older kids."

"But is she safe?" Marika asked urgently. "She's only two. Who is watching over her?"

"An older girl named Lucy. I think she's fourteen. She was still looking for her parents, too. She thought they were being held prisoner by some old lady vampire. She was on her way to try and set them free. And until Dani found her mother—you—Lucy was going to keep her by her side so she'd stay safe."

"What about Addie?" Beck interjected. "She should have been with Dani. She's an older woman, with short red hair."

"I know. She stays with Dani all the time. But a few days ago, she got sick. A man took her to the hospital."

"She let him?" Narrow-eyed, Marika chewed on one long fingernail. "I'm surprised, especially since Dani was in her care. She wouldn't just abandon her."

Again Eli looked down at his feet. "She was too sick to choose, ma'am. The man said he left her at a hospital so she could get some help."

"What hospital?" Beck asked, his voice

sharp. He already had his cell phone out, ready to call.

Eli gave a one-shoulder shrug. "I dunno. It was a big one. More than one story. I can't remember the name of the town."

"Try." Speaking through clenched teeth, Beck had to force himself to rein in his impatience. "I need to find out where she is so I can make sure she's all right."

The boy looked crestfallen. "I'm sorry, mister. I really can't remember."

"Where were they—?" Marika started to ask. A look of horror spread over her beautiful face as she slowly climbed to her feet. "Brigid." She looked at Beck. "Sweet blood of Bast, they're going to Brigid."

A quick glance at Renenet proved she was right.

"That's what I bring to the table," Renee said, a note of smugness in her tone. "If we get there before the children, we might have a chance to save them. I know Brigid's fortress inside and out. Without me, you'd be lost."

"But Brigid isn't there, right?" Beck interjected. "You said she's out searching. And—" he indicated the still frozen crowd "—the fact that she was able to influence all these people to try to capture us proves she must be somewhere close by. Or at least in the general area."

"True. But if she learns the children are coming to her, she'll simply pack up, go home and wait."

"*If.* There are a lot of *ifs* here. Too many variables."

Renee didn't reply, but then, what could she say?

Tilting her head, rubbing her temples, Marika considered. "What else, Renenet?" she asked, her voice hoarse. "Do you have magic at your command also? Magic we could use to help us if we fight Brigid?"

"I do." Renee's smile widened. "You definitely need me."

Hell, no. Beck trusted Renenet about as far as he could throw her. "What's in it for you?" he asked bluntly. "Why are you so eager to take on the most powerful vampire in the universe?"

At his harsh tone, Eli moved closer to Renee, standing so his side bumped hers. He trusted her. Interesting.

"Because I want to right a wrong." Renee

crossed her muscular arms. "I'm tired of being used."

"Plus," Marika said as she watched her closely, "I suspect you want to stage a coup, to take Brigid's spot. You wish to become High Priestess, don't you?"

Lifting her chin, Renee didn't look away. "Maybe. Can you blame me? For five hundred years, I've observed that witch. She shows no sign of growing tired, of stepping down. Instead, her hunger for power increases daily, and Goddess only knows what she'll do if she can gain control of the griffons. I suspect she wants to make them her own personal army and eventually use them against the Pack."

Beck thought the same, though he didn't agree with her entirely. Instead, he watched Eli intently. "Boy, you've yet to give your opinion on what we've talked about."

A flash of surprise crossing his face, Eli cocked his head. "I'm only a kid. Since when does what I think matter to an adult?"

Beck had to hide his smile. The boy had wisdom beyond his years. "Since now. I need your thoughts. Do you think the other children are going to Brigid?"

"I don't know," he said. "It depends on how she calls to them."

"Calls to them how?"

"You know. Magic. She can make them feel warm. Safe. Happy. Sometimes that can be kind of nice."

"With magic? Have you heard her calling?"

"Not in a while," Eli admitted, shuffling his feet. "But she did once, a while ago. I didn't like the sound of her, but the other kids, especially the younger ones, seemed to really like it."

He slid a glance toward Marika. "I think it reminded them of their mamas."

"That's okay, Eli. You did well." Ruffling his hair, Renee then looked at them and cleared her throat. "You two need to decide what you want to do." Her colorless gaze touched on Marika before lingering on Beck. "If we're going to head to Brigid's, we need to get going soon. We need to arrive before the children do."

Marika crossed her arms. "I'm still not sure I completely believe this. The consequences..."

"Brigid cares nothing about consequences."

"Do you really think Brigid is eager to start the wars up again? Even knowing the possible result—annihilation by the humans once they learn of us?"

Renee thought for a moment, then nodded. "Yes. Brigid is not in her right mind."

Impatience surging in him, Beck decided he'd had enough. "Marika." He grabbed her arm, cutting off Renenet before she could say anything else. "We need to talk. In private. Alone."

Steering her away from the other vampire, he opened his mouth, then glanced at the still-frozen crowd surrounding them. "How long will they stay like that?"

"Until I release them."

"Can they hear?"

"I don't know." Marika frowned. "Why?"

He looked back at Renenet, who still watched them intently. "Do you think anything she says is the truth?"

Her frown deepened. "I don't know."

"Do you trust her?"

"Again, I'm not sure." She swallowed. "Though I'm relatively sure that we've got to go to Brigid's. And while I'm inclined to agree with you that it'd be better if we continue alone, we might need her help."

"Probably," he conceded. "I don't like it."

"Me, either, but we can't take a chance. There's too much at stake." She glanced at the other vampire, who patiently waited. "I want to be clear on who's in charge."

"She's going to want to be the leader."

"I know. But this is my daughter. Once we rescue Dani, if Renenet takes down Brigid, she can have her spot. I really don't care."

Hearing the truth in her words, he nodded. "Do you want to tell her, or shall I?"

"I will, but I'm leaving things open. I don't want to piss off an ally."

"Speaking of allies, I'm worried about Simon."

"Why don't you try and get in contact with him again, while I talk to Renee?"

He waited while she returned to Renenet, speaking low. Finally, the other vampire nodded and waved at Beck.

"I'm going on ahead," she said. "See you two tonight at dusk?"

"Why dusk? It's not even noon yet."

Renee and the boy exchanged a glance. "The lights," she said.

"The Marfa ghost lights?"

"Yes."

"I don't understand," Marika said. "We don't have time for that."

"Wait and see." Renee's smile was warm. She waved at her escorts to follow and took Eli's hand, leading him away.

Marika cursed under her breath.

Beck put his arm around her, and she leaned into him, as though taking comfort from his warmth. For his part, he found being near her was like a powerful drug, an opiate of sorts, addictive and as necessary as breathing. He couldn't help but wonder how she'd react if he told her this. Someday, he would. When the timing was right.

Pushing herself away from him, Marika sighed. "That settles that. We'll meet up with them in the morning on the road east of here, near Mitchell Flat."

"What about them?" Beck indicated the still-frozen townspeople. "If we leave town now, once we're clear, can you release them long-distance?"

"I don't know." She gave him a wry smile. "Remember, I've never done this before. Maybe once I'm out of the area, the spell won't hold them anymore."

Walking over to a small group of people on his left, Beck circled them. Though their chests rose and fell with their breaths, they didn't even blink. "Maybe, but we can't take that chance. I don't want to leave them like this indefinitely."

"Me, either." She came up to stand by his side, close enough that her arm brushed his. "But I'm not going to release them while we're still in town. After all, they were going to capture us for Brigid."

"Or worse," he said grimly. "Come on, let's get our truck."

They hurried back to the hotel, moving swiftly through the streets crowded with immobile people, retrieved their vehicle and headed in the same direction Renee had gone on foot. Though he'd figured they might catch up to her, they saw no signs of her or her entourage.

On the outskirts of town, Beck pulled over.

"See if you can release them now." He couldn't resist touching her, a light touch, her skin soft and cool under his hand.

Her eyes dark, she rolled down her window and leaned outside, closing her eyes. Her mouth moved as she spoke silently, either casting a new spell or removing an old one.

A moment later, she sat back up and looked at him. "Done. Now we'd better get going. There are a bunch of really confused people in Marfa right now. Some of them might come looking for answers."

He nodded, keeping his hand on her shoulder, unwilling to let her go just yet. Finally, he had to, and as he put the shift into Drive and pulled out onto the highway, he glanced sideways at her.

"What do you think of Eli?"

She gazed straight ahead rather than at him, catching her bottom lip between her teeth. "I don't know. He seems a nice enough kid. Why?"

"He appears to trust Renenet. Shifter children don't usually take to vampires so easily."

Her mouth curved into a smile. "He's not an ordinary shifter."

"Still." He couldn't stand having her so close and not touching. Barreling down the road, he could only glance sideways at her, wanting a kiss and knowing he'd have to settle for a touch instead.

"Come here," he growled, patting the seat next to him. As she scooted over, he pulled her close and smoothed back her hair, tucking it behind her ear. "I don't like this. I'm still not sure about Renee, though she does have Eli to lend her story some credence."

She relaxed against him, letting him put his arm around her shoulders. "Me, either, but it's the first time we have anything concrete about Dani. And Renenet's story explains a lot of things. If the children are going to Brigid, that explains why she's made no effort to locate us."

"True, but I figured that was because she was looking for the children. I can't picture Brigid waiting in her lair for them to come to her."

"I can. She's like a spider hiding in her web."

"Maybe. But I still can't shake the feeling something's wrong. What if Renee is lying?"

"Why would she be?" She gave a one-shoulder shrug. "And wild as it seems, I like having a plan. It's better than doing nothing."

Once, he would have been the one making that statement. When had he become the man who opted for the safe way over the impetuous one?

Still, this was Brigid they were discussing. Powerful, ancient Brigid. Infiltrating her place would be like trying to sneak into the White House and play tag with the president.

"This could be a good thing," she repeated. "One thing I've learned over the centuries is that action is always better than inaction."

Hellhounds, he remembered when he would have been the one to make that statement. Now, with his experiences behind him, he had no choice but to urge caution. Running in place worked only for the very young and naive.

"Maybe, but what good are we going to be to Dani if Brigid reduces us to Jell-O?"

"True." Grim-faced, Marika turned to him. "If you have another option, then tell me."

She had him there. "I don't."

"Then I guess we have no choice but to get ready to get on the road with Renee and her group." She looked him over, her liquid gaze dark and unreadable.

"True, but she said she'd meet us there at dusk. We've got some time to kill. What do you think? Should we check out a few more water towers before we hook up with her?"

Licking her lips, she nodded. "We'll have to drive past the flats to get to Alpine."

"Yeah." He shot her a smile, hoping for one in return. "But what else are we going to do?"

"I'd like to try to contact Dani again."

"We can do that."

"We'll wait until we're close to town." Settling back in the seat, she turned her head to gaze out the window again. Cactus and scrub pines, dry earth, gulches and arroyos. And the mountains, their edges worn smooth with time.

He understood how one could lose oneself in a place like this.

When he felt her gaze on him again, he glanced at her.

"Why here?" he asked. "Why the desert?"

She rolled down her window, letting the hot, dry breeze blow her hair. "Can you not see the beauty? I love the dry earth, the cactus and the tumbleweed, and the rugged soft edges of the earth and the mountains."

"I do, too. It's stark but haunting."

"Exactly." She smiled.

With a hard look, he challenged her. "Quit

skirting the truth. It's pretty scenery, true. But there must be another reason you decided to buy a home here. Why did you choose this place to raise our daughter?"

Slowly, the smile faded from her face. "Beauty isn't enough?"

"For anyone else. But I know you. You had another reason."

Chapter 14

Marika bit her lip so hard she tasted her own blood. Dare she tell him the truth? Such a simple reason, but so revealing.

Another quick look at his rugged profile and she decided he needed to know. If Beck really wanted to be in Dani's life, he'd be in hers also.

"There's only one reason I chose to live in west Texas," she said softly. "You."

"Me? I don't follow."

"I met you here. Fell in love with you here. And, though I knew you traveled all over for your job, you always came back here to see Addie and to visit Juliet's grave."

"Me?" Disbelief threaded his voice. "You stayed here because of me?"

Face heating, she nodded.

"That makes no sense." He sounded angry. "You kept my daughter hidden, you made no move to contact me. Don't try to backpedal now."

She supposed she deserved that. "I have no reason to lie to you, not now." Swallowing, she found herself blinking back unexpected tears. "I have nothing left to gain."

"True." His harsh tone softened. "But I still don't understand why you'd choose to stay in an area for someone whom you spent the last two years avoiding like the plague."

"Maybe I was subconsciously hoping to rectify that."

"Why are you telling me this now?"

Reaching to touch him, she reconsidered and withdrew her hand. "You said you wanted truth between us, so that's what I'm giving you."

"But why now?" Honest confusion colored his voice. "In the middle of all this."

"Because," she said simply, "it needs to be said."

She took a deep breath before continuing.

"Before I met you, I was dead. Yes, I know all vampires are literally dead, but my insides, my emotions, had gradually begun to fade away. I was in true danger of becoming an automaton. Several times, I thought about ending my life— you have no idea how the years can stretch out endlessly when you have nothing to live for."

She shook her head in frustration. "I'm not doing a good job of conveying what I want to say."

"Oh, I don't know about that." Such sadness in his tone. "You've just described me to a *T*. And I haven't even lived as long as you."

This time, she reached out and squeezed his shoulder. She couldn't help but offer comfort, however small. "You used to tease me all the time, remember? You made me understand that closing yourself off from the rest of the world is no way to live."

"But you had a reason, a purpose." The words exploded from him. "You had your daughter. What about the rest of us?"

"All things come in time."

"Easy for you to say."

"No. It's not." She leaned closer, wishing she had the soul of a poet, so she could put her thoughts into words so beautiful they couldn't help but resonate in him.

"I need you," she said, meaning the words as she'd never meant anything else before.

"Marika," he groaned. "Don't do this to me. Not now."

"Then when?"

"When I'm not driving, so I can kiss you properly."

Heat rippled through her at the molten look he gave her.

Quivering, she reached out and tentatively stroked his arm.

Then, muttering a curse, he pulled the truck to the side of the road and slammed on the brakes.

As he reached for her, she met him halfway.

It was only a kiss, but oh, so much more. In that hard claiming of her mouth, he made promises and she accepted them. As his lips moved over hers, and no words passed between them, he both aroused her and gave her hope. Hope for a future untainted by hurt and hate and pain. Hope like that which she hadn't known since the first time they'd gotten together.

Hope, she reflected as he lifted his head and moved away, was a beautiful and wondrous thing.

He pulled back onto the road, and they headed into Alpine.

A thorough search of that town revealed much the same as it had in Marfa. Some curious locals, a lot of brightly dressed tourists and quaint scenery. In other words, nothing.

For Beck's sake, they stopped at a local burger joint, where he ordered two double cheeseburgers and fries and proceeded to demolish all of them while she watched, amused.

Dusk had not yet fallen by the time they'd driven to Mitchell Flat. The tourist turnoff had begun to fill up with cars in preparation for the night and the hope of seeing the famous lights.

Renee and her entourage were already there, waiting. They'd spread a blanket on the ground, claiming a spot.

Eli ran up to greet them, chattering excitedly about eating ice cream and a burger.

"I had a burger, too." Beck ruffled his hair. "It was so good, I ate two."

Eli grinned, admiration shining in his bright blue eyes.

As Renee motioned them over, he followed Beck, staring up at him with adoration.

"You've gained a fan, shifter," Renee said wryly.

Beck lowered himself to the ground, pulling Eli to sit next to him. Marika took his other side.

"Tell me about Dani." She touched the little boy's arm. "I miss my little girl so much."

He gazed up at her, clearly puzzled. "What should I tell you?"

"Just stuff." She gave him a sheepish smile. "Stuff moms want to know. What was her day like? Does she get to have fun, to play? Is she getting enough to eat?"

Nodding, his expression thoughtful, he studied her. When he finally spoke, rather than answering one of her questions, he offered his own observation. "Well, she was always singing."

"Singing?" She frowned. "What do you mean?"

"It was a puzzle," Eli said thoughtfully. "We all tried to figure out what song it was. She always sang the same thing. She kept singing about a little red caboose, over and over."

Stricken, Marika raised her hand to her mouth. She knew. The others watched while she fought emotion and gathered her composure. When she thought she had herself under control, she slowly lifted her head and began singing.

It was a children's song, about a caboose behind a train, one she'd sung to her little girl a thousand times. She sang it with the ease of long practice, her voice lilting even though tears streamed down her cheeks.

"That's it." Eli sprang to his feet, facing her. Excitement colored his voice and lit up his pale blue eyes. "That's the one Dani sang all the time. How did you know?"

"We used to sing it together," Marika said, her chest aching. "It's her favorite song."

Now Beck stood, circling around them restlessly. "I think I know how to find Dani," he declared.

"What?" They all turned to stare at him, Eli and Renee, and of course, Marika, who refused to allow herself to hope and frowned instead.

"Don't say something like that unless you mean it."

"Marika." He leaned in close, never taking

his gaze from hers. "I do mean it. I really think I know how to find Dani."

Jerking back as if he'd slapped her, she glared at him. "Not funny."

"I'm not joking."

In an instant she went from furious to quivering with eager anticipation. Balancing on the balls of her feet, she grabbed his shirt, yanking him closer. "Where is she then? If you truly know, then tell me now."

Raising a brow, he unfisted her hands from his shirt. "Easy. Take it easy."

She rocked back, chagrined. "Sorry. Still, to say something like that… You had to know what such a statement would do to me, how I'd feel. Now, tell me what you meant. Do you really think you know Dani's location?"

He gave her a gentle smile. "Not exactly."

When she opened her mouth to protest, he silenced her with a quick touch of his fingers against her lips. "I didn't say I knew where she was, but how to find her. Two different things."

She nodded, realizing that he wasn't deliberately being mysterious, just trying to gather his fragmented thoughts into a cohesive whole.

A tiny spark of hope flared inside her. Still,

she waited, aware of Renenet and Eli watching them also. Staring at him, she kept her expression tentative, as if she didn't dare to hope, as if showing any emotion at all would be sorely tempting fate.

The silence stretched on until it became unbearable.

"Well?" she asked softly. "If you have something to say, then speak."

"Even if it's only a theory?"

"Yes. Right now we have few ideas and precious little to go on. Give me your theory. It can't hurt."

He cleared his throat. "If they are indeed on the move, heading toward Brigid's, I think Dani's looking for you."

"Of course she is." She didn't bother to keep the impatience from her voice. "She's been calling me ever since they took her away."

"But she has no way to locate you."

"And?" Marika crossed her arms.

"So sing to her. She's been trying to find you. Let her use the song."

"Like a homing beacon?"

"Exactly." Leaning in, he gave her a quick

kiss, clearly able to see her hesitation. "What have you got to lose?"

"True, that." She took a deep breath and began singing, increasing the volume as her voice warmed.

A moment later, Eli joined in.

Marika held out her hand and he took it.

As she sang, she tried to project her voice, waiting for her daughter to connect.

Nothing.

Only her voice and the boy's, together with the approach of the darkness.

Some of the humans gathering in their own groups around them stared. Marika ignored them, continuing her song.

A moment later, Beck took her other hand and joined in, his deep baritone blending perfectly with hers.

Only Renenet and her two escorts abstained. They did their part though, staring down any humans who appeared about to protest. They looked so dangerous and so menacing, that none did.

Somewhere between the fifth and sixth rendition, darkness fell, swift and black and merciless. The restless crowd stilled and grew silent, yet Marika, Eli and Beck continued to sing.

From the distance, echoing off the flat, cooling desert and mysterious mountains, came a foreign sound, haunting and beautiful, as though the angels blew a magical flute to accompany the song.

"They come," Renenet whispered, staring at the darkening purple of sky. "Silence now," she said, taking Marika's arm.

Marika ignored her, continuing the song. Glancing at Beck, she wondered if he could hear their daughter singing.

Hope is found in unlikely places. The phrase kept echoing through her head as she stared at the flat plain in the growing darkness. When darkness came this far from civilization, it came like a violent death—sudden and swift, with no method of escape. The lights the gathered humans had come to see were the exception.

A single flash of gold, far off on the distant horizon, resembled molten heat lightning. Swift and violent, this couldn't be the perfect spheres those gathered had come to see.

Then the first ball of light appeared, startlingly close.

For the first time, Marika's voice faltered. Eli went silent, too, and a moment later, so did Beck.

More lights flashed into existence, increasing in both number and size.

Awestruck, the humans murmured.

"It's them," Eli said, squeezing her hand so tightly it hurt. "They're coming."

"Who?" Marika asked, almost afraid to hope. "Is it the children, or are they still on their way to Brigid?"

"Both." The boy sounded wise beyond his years. "They detoured this way because of your singing. Your song drew Dani, and, because she's the most powerful, the others let her lead the way."

"The lights, what are they?"

"Beacons to light their way. Sometimes we griffons use them as a method of travel." He grinned, reminding her he was still a child. "It's fun."

"So you think Dani is inside these lights?"

He nodded, still grinning. "I don't think

it. I know. If you listen, you can hear her calling you."

Fairly vibrating with impatience, Marika strained to calm herself enough to try, but her restlessness made her incapable of standing still.

"Do you hear?" He peered up at her, expectation shining in his face.

"No." She glanced at Beck. "What about you?"

He cocked his head. "I hear faint singing. The same song as earlier."

"That's her!" Eli jumped up and down with undisguised joy. "She knows you're here. She's on her way."

Marika exchanged a glance with Beck. Her daughter—their daughter—finally.

She took a step forward and realized that she and Beck's hands were still linked. He moved with her, and in accord they began walking away from the others, skirting the low fence and climbing between the slats, skidding down one gully and back up another, walking toward the softly glowing lights. Walking toward their daughter. Toward Dani.

Behind them, several humans called out.

"Where are you going? You're not supposed to go past the boundary. Wait. Come back."

They ignored them, confident Renee and her crew would deter any who might be foolish enough to follow.

The closer they came, the larger and brighter the hovering spheres appeared.

Suddenly, something blocked them. An invisible wall. Magic.

This could only mean one thing.

"Brigid?" Marika gasped. "Not now, not here. Not when we're so close."

"Fight it," Beck urged. "She has power, but yours is stronger. And she must be doing this from a distance."

True. The knowledge that he was correct gave her impetus. Pushing forward, she shoved against the invisible barricade with one hand, holding on to Beck with the other.

The wall fell away.

As they moved forward, three shapes flashed from the darkness to block them.

Brigid and two others had arrived.

Hands still linked, without hesitation Marika pushed past them.

"The children are mine," Brigid snarled. She

raised her hand and sent a tidal wave of power at them, pushing them to the ground. Marika fought, struggling to regain her body, but try as she might, she couldn't move.

The instant Brigid knocked them down, Beck knew the battle of the century had arrived. From somewhere, he found enough of a reserve of strength to drag his free hand to his pocket and press the GPS alert button on his cell phone. When he'd been a Protector, they'd called that the 911 button, to be used only in a life-threatening situation. Pressing it guaranteed immediate help would be dispatched.

Meanwhile, the hovering lights drifted closer. Dani's childish voice still echoed in his head.

"I won't allow you to take her," Marika spoke, gritting her teeth and straining against the invisible bounds. "Beck and I will fight you."

"Beck?" Brigid's sharp laugh felt painful on his ears. "I will take him, too. I can use him to mate with others and create more children like yours."

Somehow, Beck pushed words out of his locked mouth. "Over my dead body."

"If it comes to that." The ancient vampire sounded unruffled. "I don't need all of you to make a child. Just one part."

Roaring with rage, Beck tried to push himself to his feet, without success.

His Herculean effort didn't go unnoticed.

"Don't move." Brigid sent another shot of power at him, flattening him on the ground. "If you try that again, I will squash you like an insect."

More shapes materialized out of the darkness. Hundreds of them. From his prone position, Beck couldn't fully study them, but he could tell enough to know there were both vampires and shifters assembling.

Good. When the Protectors arrived to help him, maybe they'd have some allies. Assuming Simon sent them.

The glowing orbs continued to drift closer, until they hovered right above them. More appeared, until the night sky filled with them, appearing more golden than black, and lighting up the plateau as though by lightbulbs.

A flash of gold bathed them, and suddenly,

Brigid's spell fell away and Beck could move. Scrambling to his feet, he helped Marika up.

In the distance came the sound of a helicopter.

Reinforcements.

"The Protectors are on their way," he told Marika. "We'll need all the help we can get."

Clearly furious, Brigid's mouth worked soundlessly. Seeing she couldn't speak, one of the other vampires spoke. "You'll start another shifter-vampire war. Are you prepared for the repercussions of that?"

"If anyone starts a war, it'll be you." Marika faced her nemesis. Bathed in the golden glow, she appeared stronger, more powerful.

"I only want what's mine," Brigid snarled.

"There's nothing of yours here." Soft-voiced, Marika moved away, tugging Beck with her toward where a group of the largest globes of light were lowering themselves to the ground.

Heart pounding in his chest, he stood with her, hand in hand, watching as the glowing lights solidified and became still.

"She's here," the vampires spoke softly. "She's ours." The timbre of their voices irritated Beck like nails scraping a chalkboard.

"She can change." Among themselves, the late-arriving shifters muttered. Several gave suspicious looks to the other beings. None of them was used to working with or even coexisting with so many other species. "Because she can change, she's ours."

"She's not yours," Beck said. "She's our daughter, a little girl."

"She's all these things," Eli spoke, surprising them. He and Renenet approached. Unafraid, the young boy glanced around him at all the assembled beings. "This is a historic day."

Historic day? Beck cared nothing about any of that. He'd been denied too long—two long years, seven-hundred and thirty days had passed without him meeting his daughter. He'd heard her crying, felt her pain resonating inside his own heart, and he knew he could bring much to enhance Dani's existence.

Wisdom, steadiness, guidance and love. Most of all, love. A family. Everything he'd always wanted, everything he'd always secretly longed for but never dreamed he'd have.

"Call her," Eli said. "Call Dani out of the sphere."

As Marika opened her mouth, Beck squeezed her hand.

"Not with words. Sing to her," he told Marika, continuing to grip her hand. "Sing to all of them. Sing them home."

The approaching chopper grew closer. The globes continued to brighten, their glow intensifying.

Marika began to sing, her voice clear and strong. She sang the same children's tune about the red caboose, unwavering and lilting, a mother singing to her little girl.

One of the globes shattered, a soundless explosion of sparkling light. A tiny girl stood there, peering out at the surrounding crowd, frowning as she concentrated. Her jet-black hair fell straight to her shoulders, and Beck saw both himself and Marika in her perfect features.

"Mama!" she squealed and began running.

Marika met her halfway, scooping her up and lifting her high above her head. "Dani!" She hugged her close, tears streaming down her cheeks. "Oh, baby, I've missed you so much."

Watching this joyful reunion, a wave of emotion hit him, so strong it made Beck stagger, nearly sending him to his knees.

His mate. Their child.

Family.

A gust of wind ruffled his hair as the helicopter hovered over them. An instant later, the huge chopper began to land, setting down in a field just beyond the gathering of lights.

The assembled crowd began to murmur among themselves, shifting restlessly. Yet they didn't disperse. Instead, they continued to line the outskirts of the meadow, vampires alongside shifters, all of them watching and waiting. For what? War to break out?

And the Marfa lights grew brighter. Then, one by one, the bubbles and spheres began to disintegrate, until eleven more children stood where the lights had been.

Oblivious, Marika rained kisses on their daughter's face.

It was Dani who slowly turned, her huge brown eyes finding Beck. Her bottom lip quivered as she stared.

"Man, Mama." She pointed to Beck.

Hugging her close, Marika smiled. "That's your daddy, honey. Daddy."

"Daddy?"

Hearing her say the word in her sweet, child-ish voice brought tears to his eyes.

Afraid to hope, terrified of being rebuffed, nonetheless, he held out his arms. "Come see Daddy, sweetheart."

Dani hesitated. Then, after her mother gave her an encouraging smile, she flew across the few feet that separated them, throwing herself into his arms.

"Daddy!"

Holding her, Beck wept.

Her raven hair was soft and wavy, exactly as his had been as a young pup. She smelled of powder and some kind of citrus fruit, oranges maybe. She felt solid and strong and so very small and perfect in his arms.

A strangled curse from Marika made him look up.

Blades still softly whirling, the helicopter had completed its landing.

Beck slowly stood, giving Dani a little push to send her back to her mother. As he watched, three men jumped from the chopper, armed with assault rifles, crouched low, and began running toward them.

Chapter 15

Beck tensed, wishing like hell he had his gun.

From the corner of his eye he saw Brigid, raising her arm to send a sizzling jolt of her magic fast at them.

As she did, a second later, he recognized one of the men.

"Simon!" He instinctively started forward at the exact moment that Brigid unleashed her power, full force.

Beck took the brunt of the hit in the back. Meant for three men—no, three *shifters*—it roared through him, tearing him apart, ripping him up. The pain was swift and agonizing, but in the dim recesses of his consciousness, he knew he'd survive. Shifters could only be killed by fire or silver, and on top of that, he'd found his mate and held their daughter in his arms and looked into her eyes. For that reason alone, he'd find the strength to heal. He refused to die. He would live, damn it.

From somewhere he heard a howl of agony, and for an instant he thought he'd disgraced himself and cried out, but through a haze of red he realized the sound had come from else-where, made by a feminine voice.

Marika. Oh, sweet Jesus. Marika. And Dani.

Aware he was a gruesome sight, even as the blood flooded into his eyes and blinded him, he tried to smile, to reassure his two girls that he was okay, that even now his limbs sought to rejoin each other as his body began to swiftly heal, with shifter superspeed.

True, all of it. But that didn't stop the hurt-ing. As he fought against the pain, dimly he became aware of the crowd melting away, as though seared by heat from the blast. He saw the three armed Protectors, Simon and two others, struggling to fight free from the over-spraying remnants of Brigid's strong magic.

And then he saw Dani and Marika rushing to his side, Marika's expression full of horror and shock, Dani's bewildered. He gave silent thanks that she was too young to understand what had happened.

Marika hovered on the edge of losing herself to blind, all-encompassing panic. He knew he had to get her to regain her focus, to draw upon her inner strength, if they'd even have a prayer against Brigid.

He opened his mouth, meaning to tell her, but his throat had collapsed, and he found speaking was impossible. Urgency drove him to try. Again he failed, so instead, he tried to communicate with his eyes, to relay a desperate message, using a connection far deeper than words.

Be strong. He sent his thoughts, as clearly as he could. *Marika, you must stop Brigid. Try to help Simon. Protect Dani.*

But Marika seemed oblivious. Distracted, she wouldn't even make eye contact, futilely trying only to stop the bleeding, as though she'd forgotten how swiftly shifters healed. Any other time, he would have found this touching, proof that she still cared for him. Now though, he wanted the Huntress back.

While she tried to help him, Marika kept Dani close as though to protect her. In her panic and worry, she managed to forget utterly that Dani was no ordinary two-year-old. Dani had not only inherited her mother's powers, but developed her own. With the right direction and help, she'd be deadly. Together, the two of them could smash Brigid like an unwanted, intrusive insect.

If they didn't wait too long and lose the chance.

Still fluttering over him, Marika made little sounds of distress in her throat. She'd never looked more human or more beautiful, but more than anything he needed her to remember her nature. Vampire witch and, most importantly, Vampire Huntress, she was their best chance for survival.

Again he tried to wave Marika away, to do something to let her know he'd survive and convince her to take care of the other unfinished business.

He would be just fine. Mouth moving, he

tried again to force words up from the shattered ruin that had been his throat.

"I'm okay" he croaked. But then he smelled smoke. Turning his head, he saw the flames licking at the edge of his vision. Fire, his sole nemesis. Fire, no doubt caused by a stray spark from the chopper. The blaze grew and spread, licking at the dry desert brush, roaring into life, a furious, hungry entity, heading right toward him.

Prey.

The first frisson of sheer terror stabbed him. This could finish him, them, and he needed to do something. He was afraid, but more for his mate and their child than for himself. If any harm came to them, he'd die a thousand deaths. And also, he didn't want his baby girl to have to watch her daddy die.

He moved his mouth, mimicking the words he couldn't speak. *Go away. Move.*

Marika didn't even notice.

But Dani did.

Flashing Beck a half smile, his daughter pulled herself free from her mother and shook her head, glaring at Brigid.

"Bad lady," she said loudly, her little voice

harsh with a sternness far beyond her tender years. Shooting Beck another glance, she waved one chubby little hand, and his pain completely vanished.

A wiggle of her plump fingers, and his body was made whole, without even a single bruise, cut or bump.

Unreal. Like a healer of Halflings. Beck had heard of a woman in central Texas who could do such things.

Then, while everyone was still reeling from the unexpected turn of events, Dani clapped her hands. An instant later, the fire vanished, as if it had never existed. Not even a puff of smoke or charred ash remained.

A miracle. Beck didn't waste a second more in examination. He jumped to his feet, just in time to watch his little girl twist and slip from her mother's arms. She marched up to the fierce, ancient vampire and faced her, unafraid, with her tiny hands on her small hips.

Several of the onlookers gasped. Beck tried to make his legs move, but his feet felt glued in place, unable to take a single step.

In a flash, Marika stood. Huntress. He knew the exact instant she tapped in to her magic.

She appeared to swell, though her size remained exactly the same. Grabbing her, Beck attempted to hold her back.

Gently, without looking at him, she peeled his fingers away, removed his grip. This done, she strode forward, pushing in front of her daughter, shielding the little girl with her own body.

"Prepare to fight, Brigid," she said, the power in her voice echoing off the mountains. "You don't touch what is mine."

Brigid laughed, the dark sound sending chills down Beck's spine. "You dare to challenge me, Huntress? I can destroy you with one wave of my hand."

Pushing in front of her mother, Dani rushed forward.

"Dani, no. Stop." Marika went for her child. The two-year-old neatly sidestepped her, focused only on their nemesis.

"Dani, come back," Beck cried, his heart pounding. Marika glanced at him, their gazes touched, and he knew she was thinking the exact same thing. If anything happened to their baby...

Nothing would.

Marika made another attempt to grab the little girl. And once again, Dani evaded her. She marched right up to Brigid, her small face red with fury.

"You hurt my daddy."

Marika froze.

Hearing the rage in Dani's high-pitched voice, Brigid laughed, clearly amused. One elegantly shaped brow rose as she looked down her nose at the toddler. "Maybe I did," she allowed, her voice condescending. "So what?"

"I don't like that."

She crouched down, until she was nose to nose with Dani. "Since there's nothing you can do about it, why don't you come with me and save your father from any more pain?"

"She's staying with me, Brigid," Marika said before Dani could reply, her voice fierce and determined as she rushed forward and grabbed her baby's arm. "Leave her the hell alone."

She might as well not have spoken. Both Brigid and Dani ignored her.

Still glaring fiercely up at the vampire, Dani shook off her mother's hand and wrinkled her small, freckled nose, as though she smelled something awful. She blinked, whispered something and waved her hand. Brigid went flying backward, slamming into the side of the chopper and narrowly missing getting sliced in two by the still-rotating blades.

Everyone—vampires, shifters and the odd assorted humans—froze, gawking at where Brigid sprawled motionless on the ground.

Everyone except the children. They swarmed around Dani and Marika, exclaiming over the sight of Dani's mother, since they'd heard so much about her. They crowded close, reaching out with small hands to touch her hair, her skin, and clamoring for her attention.

Keeping an eye on Brigid to make sure she didn't move, Marika allowed this with a slight smile, though she also watched Dani, who viewed her friends and her mother with a slightly amused, indulgent smile. Beck noticed Marika was balanced on the balls of her feet, in case Brigid got up ready for another round and her Huntress side was needed.

His girls. Beck thought his chest would explode from pride. Slowly, testing joints that should have felt pain, he cautiously took one step, then another. Nothing. He had been completely healed.

Relieved to learn his legs already worked, he moved over to stand with his mate, motioning their daughter to join them.

Meanwhile, an enraged Brigid scrambled to her feet, murder in her eyes, and started forward, only to be grabbed by Simon and another Protector. They held her, one on each side, with the third Protector keeping his weapon aimed at her head.

Blowing her brains out then ripping her apart would certainly kill her.

Motionless, even Brigid appeared to recognize that.

"I did not give you permission to touch me. Release me immediately," she ordered, baring her fangs as she gathered her strength. Gun or no gun, apparently she made ready to cast a spell that would blow them into oblivion. "Or I'll—"

With a curse, Marika straightened. Beck could see her gathering her magic in preparation for another battle.

"No," little Dani said, stamping her feet. Her high-pitched, childish voice rang with adult firmness. "Leave everyone alone, mean lady. Go away."

Brigid opened her mouth to speak, perhaps to protest, maybe to cast her spell, but before she could, Dani waved three chubby fingers and poof! Brigid simply vanished, leaving the Protectors holding nothing but air.

The crowd, obviously stunned by the rapid progression of events, stared and began murmuring among themselves.

"What did you do to her?" Renee asked, expression both troubled and awed.

Dani lifted her chin, once more looking like a normal, mischievous two-year-old again. "I sent her bye-bye."

"Where?" Renee wanted to know. Beck figured that was so she could determine how long before the Vampire Priestess returned.

"To the place with the lions and tigers. And snakes. She can bother them now." She giggled in obvious delight. "If she's mean, they'll eat her."

Spoken with the logic of a toddler. Beck and Marika exchanged a look. Had Brigid been sent to Africa or only to a zoo in some big city like El Paso, Dallas or Houston?

He started to ask, then thought better of it. They'd worry about that later. For now, they still had the assembled crowd of Brigid supporters to deal with.

Though, as he eyed the still-shocked group, none of them looked even mildly threatening. Indeed, some of them began to wander off on their own, dazed and wanting only to leave the volatile scene behind them.

Eli trotted over, beaming so brightly his freckles glowed, and hugged Dani. Releasing her, he then turned to face the remainder of Brigid's immediate entourage, keeping one slender hand still on Dani's tiny shoulder.

"Anyone else?" he asked quietly. "We need to know now. If you have something to say to us, better say it now."

Though several shifted from foot to foot uneasily, no one answered. Marika visibly relaxed, apparently banishing her Huntress side and allowing herself to just be a mother again. A mother, Beck thought, loving her so much it hurt, the mother of his precious daughter and, perhaps more importantly, his mate.

"Good." Eli scrutinized them one more time. "Please, we're just little kids." He gave them all a gap-toothed grin.

"What do you want?" Marika asked softly, her expression gentle.

"We want our moms and dads and our sisters and brothers." His smile wavered. "We're all sick and tired of running and hiding and grown-ups trying to control us. We want our families."

The words resonating in him, Beck stared, the old familiar ache starting. Families. Something he'd never had. He'd been taken by the Society of the Protectors when he was four, and shortly thereafter, his parents had been killed in a car crash. From then on, unlike most of the other boys in the Protector Training school, he never left. Not for holidays or breaks or vacations. He'd had nothing else.

The Protectors called themselves brothers, but Beck knew he was different. Unlike all the other guys, he'd never had a real family.

Until now. Marika and Dani. His family. And, if they'd let him into their inner circle, from this point on, he meant to make them his entire life.

And there was one more person. Someone who meant the world to him. But, though he searched the crowd, he didn't see her face.

"Where is Addie?" he demanded. "Does anyone know anything about Addie?"

"She's probably still in the hospital," Eli said. "She was very sick."

Marika hastened to reassure him. "I'm sure she'll call us when she can."

If she can, he thought, though he kept the correction to himself. He had to find Addie, to make sure she was okay. When this was all over, he'd search for her. Until then, he could only hope that his longtime friend wasn't dead or dying.

"We want our families," Eli repeated.

Several of the children murmured their agreement with Eli's words.

"We'll do everything we can to locate your parents," Simon said. "We'll need to talk to each of you individually." He pointed to the other two men. "Each of us will take four of you. I'll take the fifth."

Watching as the children lined up, Eli made no move to join them. He looked alternatively proud and scared. A moment later, Beck learned why.

"Eli, you don't have a family." Renee's voice, sounding uncertain for the first time since he'd met her. She moved closer, stopping a few feet away from him. Her normal haughty expression looked vulnerable.

"Nope." He made an attempt to smile. "I've got no one to be returned to, so there's no point in me getting in line."

Renee stared, her eyes glowing. Swallowing audibly, she took a deep breath before she spoke. "Since you don't, I was wondering if, that is, I mean, maybe you'd like to live with me? We could be each other's family."

A shifter raised by a vamp? Beck saw several others of his kind about to protest and glared them down. Marika did the same with the vampires. Maybe the time had come for them all to adjust their perceptions of other species.

"Live with you?" Eli stared up at her, looking both frightened and exhilarated, all at once. "Are you sure?"

Renee nodded fiercely, her eyes suspiciously bright. "I promise I'll make sure you're schooled in the ways of the Pack."

At those words, several of the shifters relaxed, smiling and nodding. The vampires, though they didn't look happy, resumed their normal, blasé expressions.

Renee was the exception. She didn't move. Face hopeful, she intently watched the boy, waiting for him to decide with a combination of anticipation and fear.

They stared at each other, and then, with a glad cry, Eli ran to her, wrapping his arms around her legs and holding on tight.

Smoothing his hair, Renee gave Beck a brilliant smile. "I took the risk," she said. "And got what I most wanted. Now it's your turn."

His turn? Blind panic flashed through him as everyone turned to eye him, including Marika. The question in her beautiful eyes made him want to kiss her, hard and fast and deep, but from the corner of his eye he saw Simon motioning him over, one hand on a tall, thin boy's shoulder.

"Later," he mouthed, before going to assist his friend.

Dazed at the rapid turn of events, Marika held her precious child close and struggled to hang on to her shredded self-control.

Huntress she might be, but right now in this

moment in time, she was a mother first. And her baby girl was all that mattered.

Her baby girl...and Beck. The father of her child and her mate.

Renee had told him it was his turn to take a risk. She wondered what that had been all about.

Holding Dani tight, she watched him with Simon and the children. Though she searched his beloved face for an answer, she found nothing.

Later, after the children had been loaded into the chopper to go to El Paso, Beck rejoined Marika. Dani had fallen asleep in her mother's arms. Marika had wrapped her in a blanket and was letting her doze.

For a moment Beck gazed down at his sleeping daughter, his expression hidden. When he turned his head to look at Marika, the bleakness in his eyes made her ache.

"Simon found Addie," he told her, sounding remote. "She was transferred to a hospital in El Paso in severe respiratory distress."

Small talk, small talk. She could do that. "What's wrong with her?"

"She had pneumonia. But she's all better

now. I talked to her and Addie's made a complete recovery. Simon's having her flown home tomorrow."

He should have sounded happy, relieved, or something. Anything would have been preferable to this detached, robotic man.

Peering up at him, she wondered if he'd gone into shock. She thought of Renee's words and decided to repeat them back to him.

"It's your turn to take a risk."

His eyes flashed. Pain or sorrow, or some other deep emotion. What, she couldn't say.

"How do you know that?" His face still looked the same, almost vampirelike in its complete and utter lack of expression.

Though she felt a flash of recognition—how well she knew that form of retreating—she refused to back down.

This was too important. Every Vampire Huntress knew once the hunt had been started, it had to continue.

To do any less was more than foolish. It was death.

Something of her thoughts must have shown in her face. Beck smiled. "I've never been a coward," he said. "But this, I want this so

badly. I honestly don't know how I'll feel if—"
He stopped, bowing his head to gaze at their
daughter.

"If?" she prodded gently, ninety-nine percent sure she knew what he was about to say.
So many times she'd told him she didn't want
him around, and never once realized she was
lying to herself and to him. He had the right to
know—and love—their daughter.

Now would be the time to rectify her mistake. "It's okay, Beck. I'd really like you to be
a part of Dani's life."

"What about yours?" he rasped.

"Mine?" Momentarily confused, she didn't
know what else to say or do, so she resorted to
her vampire stoniness.

Then he raised his head, and his eyes blazed
with so much emotion, she crumbled. Gasping,
humbled, she suddenly realized what he was
trying to say.

"You want *me?*" She had to ask, had to be
sure.

"You—and Dani—are everything I've
always wanted…." His voice broke, as if he
found it difficult to say what he wanted to say.

For one horrifying moment, she thought he

was trying to tell her goodbye. Foolish woman, she chided herself.

Then he looked at her, letting her see the love plain on his face, and she knew she was wrong. Completely, utterly wrong. Thank the goddess.

Again he glanced at their little girl, a half smile playing on his lips, before taking both her hands in his.

"I should have done this the first time," he muttered. "So many wasted years."

Then, dropping to one knee in front of her, he kissed both her hands, his mouth lingering.

"Marika, I can't live without you. Will you do me the honor of—"

Before he could finish, she dropped down with him, so they'd be equal.

"You don't even have to ask," she said, then sealed the bargain with a kiss.

* * * * *

A sneaky peek at next month...

NOCTURNE™

BEYOND DARKNESS...BEYOND DESIRE

My wish list for next month's titles...

In stores from 18th November 2011:

☐ Guardian Wolf — Linda O. Johnston

☐ Heiress to a Curse — Zandria Munson

In stores from 2nd December 2011:

☐ Lord of the Wolfyn — Jessica Andersen

Available at WHSmith, Tesco, Asda, Eason, Amazon and Apple

Just can't wait?

MILLS & BOON® Book Club

Free Book!

Get your free books now at
www.millsandboon.co.uk/freebookoffer

Or fill in the form below and post it back to us

THE MILLS & BOON® BOOK CLUB™—HERE'S HOW IT WORKS: Accepting your free books places you under no obligation to buy anything. You may keep the books and return the despatch note marked 'Cancel'. If we do not hear from you, about a month later we'll send you 3 brand-new stories from the Nocturne™ series, two priced at £4.99 and a third, larger version priced at £6.99 each. There is no extra charge for post and packaging. You may cancel at any time, otherwise we will send you 4 stories a month which you may purchase or return to us—the choice is yours. *Terms and prices subject to change without notice. Offer valid in UK only. Applicants must be 18 or over. Offer expires 28th February 2012. **For full terms and conditions, please go to www.millsandboon.co.uk/termsandconditions**

Mrs/Miss/Ms/Mr (please circle)

First Name

Surname

Address

Postcode

E-mail

Send this completed page to: Mills & Boon Book Club, Free Book Offer, FREEPOST NAT 10298, Richmond, Surrey, TW9 1BR

Find out more at
www.millsandboon.co.uk/freebookoffer

Visit us Online

0611/T1ZEE

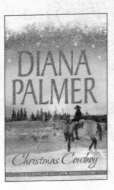

Have Your Say

*You've just finished your book.
So what did you think?*

We'd love to hear your thoughts on our 'Have your say' online panel
www.millsandboon.co.uk/haveyoursay

- 🌹 Easy to use
- 🌹 Short questionnaire
- 🌹 Chance to win Mills & Boon® goodies